Unforgettable
Book 2

Unforgettable

BOOK TWO

NELLE L'AMOUR

Nelle L'Amour thanks you for your understanding and support. To join my mailing list for new releases, please sign up here: http://eepurl.com/N3AXb

NICHOLS CANYON PRESS
Los Angeles, CA USA

Unforgettable Book 2
By Nelle L'Amour

Cover by Arijana Karcic, Cover It! Designs
Proofreading by Mary Jo Toth
Formatting by BB eBooks

For all my readers.
You are the reason I write.

"Somehow you will never know the value of a moment until it becomes a memory."

—Dr. Seuss

Unforgettable
Book 2

Chapter 1

Brandon

I haven't left Zoey's side. When I found out yesterday she was taken to the hospital, I canceled my dinner date with Katrina and rushed to Cedars. Needless to say, my fiancée wasn't happy. In fact, she was furious. How dare I bale out of her birthday because of some stupid bump on the head!

Actually, it's more than just a little bump. An MRI showed Zoey sustained a serious concussion when she fainted at The Farmer's Market. The doctors don't know what caused her to pass out. Thank God, there's no major brain damage. She's going to be okay.

I've had the hospital upgrade her to a luxurious private suite. If her insurance doesn't cover it, I'll take care of the exorbitant cost. I can easily afford it, and she deserves the best. As I vigilantly watch over her from an armchair beside her bed, a sense of déjà vu washes over me.

Only a few weeks ago, I was in a similar suite attached to all kinds of beeping machines. Lying in a life or death coma for two weeks following a hit and run accident that occurred near my house. When I finally woke up, I was surrounded by a film crew and Katrina in my face. The scene was pure chaos, my memory loss only making it worse.

Zoey is hooked up only to a single monitor that's tracking her heartbeat. There are no IVs. And there's only me. By the time I learned of her accident and got here, she was fast asleep. Her primary doctor told me she'd regained consciousness briefly and was screaming out for her father. Hysterical. In shock. Maybe even delusional as she mentioned just yesterday morning in a confrontation with my manager, Scott Turner, that her father died fighting a wildfire. They had to sedate her, and she's been in a deep sleep ever since.

I study her. I've never seen her asleep before. Morning sunlight floods the room and bathes her face in a halo. She looks like an angel, her chestnut hair fanned out on the pillow, her sensuous lips parted slightly, her long-lashed eyes gently fluttering. So close to her, I extend my arm, and with my fingertips, I trace her jaw. Her flawless alabaster skin is like velvet. And then irresistibly, I run my forefinger across her kissable lips, drawing me to her like a magnet.

Her eye flutters intensify, and a second before my

lips touch down on hers, she starts thrashing and screaming. I hastily pull away.

"Mama! Mama! Wake up!"

Crying hysterically, she must be having a bad dream. Tears stream down her tormented face as she claws at the sheets.

"Please don't shoot me! Please, please, please, please."

Her desperate, frightened cries freak me out. I don't know what to do—how to comfort her or calm her down. Maybe I should call for a nurse or a doctor. Just as I'm about to hit the call button, she bolts up, drenched in sweat and tears. And still sobbing.

I instantly move to the edge of her bed and take her into my arms. She buries her head against my chest. Her heaving breasts rest against my pecs, and her tears saturate the fabric of my T-shirt. I stroke her damp hair and try to calm her down.

"Shh, Zoey. I'm here. Everything's okay."

She lifts her head and gazes up at me with her big, wet chocolate eyes that glisten like crystals. "Brandon, I saw the man who shot my mother."

"What do you mean, baby?" The last word inadvertently slips out, but she doesn't react to it.

In a small tearful, staccato voice, she launches into her story. I listen to every word, stunned and silent.

"On my fifth birthday, my mama took me to the Santa Monica Pier to celebrate. She knew how much I loved all the rides. And that day, I got to go on the big rollercoaster for the first time. She let me do it twice with her, and then afterward, we got corndogs and went to the edge of the pier to look for dolphins."

She blinks several times as if she's going back in time. As if she's there again. "Did your father go with you?"

She shakes her head and confirms what she revealed yesterday. "No. He died two years earlier putting out a wildfire. He was a fireman."

"I'm sorry." My voice is soft and compassionate.

"It's okay. I don't remember him too well. But Mama I can never forget."

"Did you see any dolphins?" I ask, brushing a strand of hair off her face and eager to hear more of the story.

With a sniffle, she nods. "I was so excited and pointed them out to her. But she didn't hear me because..." Another sniffle and she bravely resumes. "Because she was slumped over the railing uncon- scious. Blood was all over the back of her sundress. No matter what I did, she didn't respond. I knew something was terribly wrong, but wasn't sure what had happened, and desperate, asked this creepy man, who was standing next to me, for help. Except when I turned to him, he collapsed to the ground bleeding profusely. I screamed, spinning around for someone to come to our aid. And then I saw him."

While I picture the terrifying scene in my head, Zoey begins to visibly shake. Her mouth quivers. I clasp the trembling hand that's not hooked up to the monitor and ask: "Who, Zoey?"

"The monster who shot the man … and Mama. He was pointing a gun at me. He fired—and missed—and then he ran away. I'll never forget his face."

My heart in my throat, I swallow hard. "Did anyone else see him?"

She shakes her head again. "The pier was very crowded and noisy. And an orchestra was playing. I'm pretty sure the gun had a silencer."

"Your mother—"

"Oh, Brandon, it was so terrible. After the man ran away, I turned back to check on her. She was no longer there. I searched the pier everywhere. And then I looked down and screamed. She'd fallen over the railing into the ocean below. She'd regained consciousness, but she didn't know how to swim. Added to that, the ocean was very rough. While the waves tossed her about, she reached for me, but I couldn't help her."

I suddenly understand her fear of swimming and brush away more tears with the pads of my fingertips before she bows her head. In my heart, I know this story's going to end like a Shakespeare tragedy.

"Brandon, I watched her drown. She went under and then a giant wave carried her out to sea." Sobs wrack her body. "I never saw her again."

Her story guts me. It was bad enough losing my parents in a horrific car accident at the age of seventeen. But how beyond awful for a fatherless little girl to watch her beloved mother bleed to death and then drown. My empathy morphs into rage. It seeps deep into my bloodstream. I want to find the bastard who did this to her and kill him with my own hands. Hold his head underwater until his soul goes to hell. I inwardly shudder. Not just at the intensity of my anger, but at the other powerful emotions that swarm me. When did I start caring so much about my assistant? Enough to want to kill for her? Have I always? I can't remember.

"Brandon, I'll never forget that man's face," she sobs out, looking up and hurtling me out of my disquieting thoughts. "Never!"

"Shh." I swipe away more tears and then steady her by cupping her trembling shoulders. "What happened afterward?" I want to know if the bastard ever paid for what he did. I'm still crazy with rage and thirsting for revenge.

Zoey sniffles, her shoulders still heaving and the tears still falling. Her voice is watery. "Mama's brother and his wife took me in…Uncle Pete and Auntie Jo."

Pete…Jo? She answers my question before I ask it.

"You know Uncle Pete. He's the detective working your hit and run case."

Yeah, I quickly figured that out. Why didn't she tell me this before? This is not the time to ask. Frankly, I'm not sure if she's ever told me about her past or her family because of my amnesia. While some memories have broken through, this one hasn't. Right now, it's all news to me.

Zoey gazes up at me. Her eyes flicker with desperation. "I need to see my father and talk to him."

I was told by the medics that he was contacted, but he's out of town with his wife at some convention until Wednesday. I share this information with Zoey and then add softly, "You should call him later when you're rested." *And coherent.* She obviously had some kind of seizure while reliving her mother's murder. I have a feeling she's still in a state of shock.

"No, I want to talk to him, now! I've got to!" my assistant chokes out, straining her hoarse voice. "Give me my phone!" Her eyes dart madly around the room. "Shit! Where's my phone?"

She grows agitated. Her head twists left and right and then she tears off the bed covers. She searches beneath them, paddling her beautiful hands like a puppy digging for a buried bone. She begins to pant. Then, hyperventilates. Fuck. I've set her off. Another round of hysteria is building.

"Here. Use mine." Reaching into my jeans pocket, I hand her my cell. Chewing on her quivering bottom lip, she hastily punches in a number. Tears are still streaming down her cheeks and her fingers are jittery. I can hear the other phone ringing.

"Dammit," she splutters. "He's not picking up." Breathing heavily, she leaves an urgent message. "Pops, please call me back on this phone or mine. It's an emergency. I saw Mama's killer!" Still frantic, she ends the call and tosses my phone on the bed.

"Brandon, I need to speak to Scott to find out why he was with Mama's killer."

Thinking she's had some kind of hallucinatory episode that landed her in the hospital, I'm taken aback. My eyes widen with surprise, "Zoey, what are you talking about?"

"I saw Scott with the man who murdered Mama at The Farmer's Market."

"Are you sure?" My voice is full of doubt. She's just thrown a curve ball my way.

"Please, Brandon, you have to believe me. I'd never forget his face. Never!"

She gazes at me with a mixture of hope and urgency. While I'm not a hundred percent sure she did, I tell her I believe her just to keep her calm. And then a familiar nasal voice captures my attention.

"Jesus, Brandon. I've been looking all over for you. Katrina told me I could find you here."

Scott!

Before I can say a word, Zoey leaps out of the bed, breaking free of the portable monitor. "Scott, what were you doing with that man at The Farmer's Market yesterday?"

My manager narrows his beady eyes, one of which twitches. "What the hell are you talking about?"

Zoey's voice rises several octaves and her eyes flare. "You were there! I saw you talking to a man with pockmarked skin and a broken nose!"

Scott turns to me. "Does she have some kind of head injury?"

Zoey shrieks. "Don't lie to me, you fucking slime-dog! You were there!" Red with rage, she bolts over to Scott and, with her white-knuckled fists, begins to pound him. "You fucking, fucking liar."

"Christ, Brandon. Get this hallucinatory psycho bitch off me."

An intervention. Clamping Zoey around the waist, I try to pull her away from my manager. She resists, pounding him harder. "No, leave me alone!! He's lying!!"

I finally force her away. In defeat, she sobs louder, hunched over and heaving. She's close to collapsing. I'm virtually holding her up. Her lifeline.

Softly, I say, "C'mon, Zoey. Hold on to me."

Depleted of energy and will, she clutches me and lets me usher her back to the bed. I get her tucked in.

"Liar!" she croaks one more time.

I turn to face Scott. "Scott, I think it best you leave."

He scoffs at me. "Call me when you're done with the nutjob." He pivots and stalks out the door. I take a seat once again on the edge of Zoey's bed. My body is turned so I'm facing her. Her sobs have grown softer, and with her forlorn eyes, she looks at me imploringly.

"Brandon, please tell me you believe me." Her rasp is another desperate plea.

I have no choice. I say yes because I don't want to upset her.

"Thank you."

"Come here." I gently take her into my arms once more, her tears ripping me apart.

"Thank you," she whispers again.

She can't forget; I can't remember. What an odd couple we make. But at this moment, holding her in my arms, we're kindred spirits, united through the loss of our parents by water and fire.

Chapter 2

Zoey

I'm released from the hospital later in the afternoon. After spending time on the set of his TV series, *Kurt Kussler,* Brandon comes by to pick me up and accompanies me as I'm wheeled out a secret entrance to the hospital that's reserved for celebrities and VIPS. He helps me into his Hummer. Though the painkillers have numbed my excruciating headache, I still feel queasy and uneasy. Totally shaken. Mama's killer is out there! Scumbag Scott! His lie is eating at me, making every cell in my body sizzle with rage. Thankfully, I finally got to talk to Pops. He believed me. I knew he would, and he's already started an investigation. As soon as he's back in town, he's going to stop by to see me.

With minimal traffic, we get to Brandon's house in no time. He pulls the scarlet Hummer into the garage next to his Lamborghini, jumps out, and rounds the monstrous SUV to open my door. I undo my seatbelt and the next thing I know I'm in his arms.

"What are you doing?"

"Carrying you. What does it look like I'm doing? The doctors want you to take it easy and stay off your feet as much as possible for the next couple of days."

"I think I can walk," I protest as he kicks open the door to his house.

"Trust me, you can't."

The truth is I secretly love every minute of being back in his strong arms. He makes me feel safe and protected. And like a waif. My arms circle his broad shoulders as he enters the kitchen.

"Wait! Where are you taking me?" I ask when I realize he's not heading to the back doors that open to the patio and lead to the guesthouse where I reside.

"You're sleeping here for the next forty-eight hours so I can keep an eye on you. I'm setting you up in one of my guest bedrooms. It has an adjacent bathroom."

"But I need my things!"

"Don't worry. I'll retrieve your personal items," he says, carrying me into the spacious guest room. Like the rest of the house, it's furnished in high-end contemporary furniture in muted shades of lavender and gray. He sets me down on the inviting four-poster steel bed. Slipping off my shoes, he insists I get under the covers and helps tuck me in. Sitting up, I'm supported by a mountain of fluffy white pillows that coordinate with the delicious down comforter.

"Don't move. I'll be right back. I'm going to get your things."

"Don't forget my toothbrush and deodorant."

He winks at me. "Don't worry."

"And some clothes."

Oh, Jeez. Why did I say that? He may go through my underwear drawer and see my big girl panties. Yikes!

"Brandon, I'm fine with what I'm wearing."

He smirks at me. "You need a little more but not much."

Brandon orders in lunch—comforting chicken soup for the soul—from Greenblatt's, our nearby deli on Sunset. Making bowls for the two of us, he agrees to let me get out of bed and screen some rough cuts of the latest episodes of *Kurt Kussler*. Snuggling on his couch so close to him takes my mind off my recent ordeal. The show looks amazing, and the story's on fire. The plot isn't the only thing heating up; his body brushes against mine and incites me. A barrage of tiny bolts of lightning bombards me.

"What's going to happen between Kurt and Mel?" I ask him. While subtle, things have been simmering between the tormented ex-CIA agent and his faithful assistant.

A coy smile lights up his gorgeous face. He shrugs. "Don't know."

Bullshit. I want to punch him. By that smug expression on his face, I so know he knows. He's after all writing the season finale. As the end credits roll, the smartass clicks the TV off and reprimands me.

"Eat!"

I look down at my bowl. So wrapped up with the episode, I've hardly touched my soup. I shift, and as I do, my spoon tumbles out of the bowl and falls to the gleaming wood floor. *Clink!*

"Shit," I mumble under my breath as I bend over to retrieve it. Except Brandon gets there at the same time. His face is in my face, just a breath away. My pulse speeds up as his long tapered fingers graze mine. Tingles course through me like bubbly champagne.

"I've got it," I say, clasping the handle and straightening up as he does.

"I'll get you a new one."

"Don't bother. My mama told me you can kiss away germs."

"Mine did too." With a smile and a twinkle in his eyes, he grasps my wrist and lifts my hand to his lips. My eyes never leave him as he kisses the back of the spoon. The way he does it is so damn sexy. With smoldering eyes and a sensuous pucker. Before my heart beats out of my chest, he releases his lips and my hand.

"You can never be too safe. On the other hand, no risk, no gain."

"Right," I reply, eyeing the little bit of saliva he's left behind on the spoon tip.

On my next sip of soup, I can taste him. The warmth of the broth heats me up further. My temperature rises and I can feel his eyes on me.

"Why didn't you tell me Pete was your father?"

I shrug and tell him the truth. "Honestly, I thought you knew."

"Actually, I didn't." He pauses. "Well, at least as far back as I can remember."

Damn his amnesia. I still haven't decided if it's better to remember or to forget. While my legs stay curled under me, my gorgeous boss stretches his long muscular limbs across the coffee table. My eyes travel down his perfectly ripped jeans to his bare feet. They're so fucking perfect. Just the right length and width. Sizeable, manly, beautifully arched with just the slightest dusting of dark hair on the instep. The girls in my massage classes used to tell me you can tell a lot about a man, especially his cock, by his feet. They were so right. A fluttery sensation erupts between my thighs as I picture Brandon's gorgeous organ. That thick, breathtaking tower of magnificence. A monument to mankind just like his feet. His virile voice cuts into my wicked ruminations.

"Why don't you and Pete have the same last name?"

"While Pete and Auntie Jo adopted me and I'm officially their daughter, I wanted to keep my last name out of respect to my real mother and father. I call Uncle Pete Pops, but I could never call Auntie Jo anything close to Mama. I'm lucky though. I couldn't ask for better parents. I'm super close to both of them and their son, who I grew up with and adore."

Brandon blows on a tablespoon of the hot soup. "What was your real father like?"

"Mama told me he was handsome and brave." I reach for my nearby bag and pull out my wallet. I flip through the pictures. "Here's a photo of the two of them taken just before he died."

Brandon studies the photo. "They were a great-looking couple. You're the best of both of them."

Brandon's right. I have my father's big brown eyes and wavy chestnut hair and my mother's porcelain skin and her full Cupid's bow lips. But unfortunately, not her fine-boned frame. Instead, I inherited Papa's big-boned, sturdy build. Well, with the exception of his hands. I glance down at my slender, long-fingered hands that are exactly like Mama's and thank Brandon for what I construe as a compliment.

"What was your mother like?" he asks.

A collage of images flashes through my head. Oh, my beautiful Mama with her wild red hair and delicate features! Where do I begin?

"She was angelic. This photo barely does her justice. Despite the fact we weren't rich, she had a lot of style and great taste. I guess you'd say, Bohemian chic. She knew how to make cheap vintage finds from flea markets look like a million bucks."

"Do you still have some of her clothes?"

"Yes, but they don't fit me." I laugh lightly. "On special occasions, I wear some of the jewelry my father saved up to buy her and use her beaded handbags." My voice chokes up. "Sadly, her wedding ring and band, which she never took off, were lost at sea."

Brandon runs a finger from my cheek to my chin. "So, your parents were in love?"

The affectionate gesture brings awareness to the pulsing bundle of nerves between my legs. I quirk a small smile.

"Totally. My father was my mother's one and only. The love of her life. Her hero. Mama cried for days when he died in that wildfire. I think if she'd lived, she would have never remarried. That's how great their love was."

Brandon takes in a deep breath. "My parents were the same way. Sometimes I think perishing together was a blessing. They never had to suffer the pain of loss."

I detect sadness in Brandon's voice, an emotion I've never witnessed. And his eyes look forlorn. "They died in a car crash, right?"

"Yeah. Some motherfucker in a van went through a red light. He didn't suffer a scratch, but both my parents died upon impact. My mother was decapitated."

"Oh my God!" I gasp. "That's horrible!" Though I read a little about the fatal crash online, I didn't know the sordid details. Resisting the urge to comfort him physically with a hug or the mere touch of my hand, I ask him if his parents' untimely and violent demise affected him.

"A lot. I was angry at the world. I wanted to kill that bastard who ran into them. He served some time, but he should have rotted in hell."

"How did you get over it?"

"I moved to LA and funneled my pain and anger into acting. It was a release."

"You studied with the legendary Bella Stadler, right?"

He blinks his eyes several times in rapid succession as if remembering something.

"Are you having some kind of memory break-through?" His mind is definitely elsewhere, and he doesn't answer me. "Brandon, are you okay?"

His eyes continue to flutter, and then he responds. "Yeah, I'm good. Bella was an amazing woman. She made me the actor ... and the man I am today."

I process his words. I recall reading somewhere that Bella was rumored to have affairs with many of her talented, handsome protégés. Did Brandon sleep with his teacher? His master? I refrain from asking and instead give him a compliment.

"You're a really good actor, Brandon."

He cocks a brow, as if in disbelief. "Really? You think so?"

I smile at him warmly, touched by what I think is a genuine, humble moment of self-doubt. "I know so. Hel-lo-O. You won the Golden Globe."

"But still. I don't think I'm a Brando. Or anywhere close to Connery."

He's referring to Marlon Brando and Sean Connery, his two favorite actors according to Wiki. I once read all actors are insecure. Even the best. I guess he's no different. My gorgeous, bigger than life action-hero boss, *People Magazine's* "Sexiest Man Alive," is just human. The egotistical asshole is actually quite adorable with his insecurity complex. I look deep into his eyes.

"Brandon, you're as good as they are. In fact, better. One day you're going to win an Oscar."

That sexy lopsided smile plays on his lips. "You're just kissing my ass."

I wish. The thought of my lips on those perfect buns of steel makes my heart skip a beat and my skin heat. "No, I'm telling you the truth."

His smile widens. "If and when I do win, I'm going to thank you."

I twitch back a small, melancholic smile. His fiancée, America's stunning "It Girl," Katrina Moore will be there when he does.

"Do you believe in happily ever after?" I think back to my erotic Cinderella dream and wonder if there's such a thing.

Brandon's smile falls from his face and his brows furrow as if in deep thought. "I don't know. Even with finding a great love, happily ever after may not exist."

My heart clenches. So, Katrina *is* his great love? A pang of jealousy stabs me.

"What do you mean?" I ask shakily.

"Just look at our parents. They never got theirs. A happily ever after ending is not promised to everyone because tomorrow isn't promised to anyone."

His profound, wistfully spoken words sink into me. I stare at his face with those beautiful long-lashed sad violet eyes and reality jabs me. Chances are happily ever after will never be mine.

In my emotionally fragile state, it's difficult to hold back tears. I set my soup bowl on the coffee table and then my cell phone rings. I pick it up and check the caller ID. It's Jeffrey. I spoke to him briefly at the hospital earlier this afternoon while Brandon was at the set and filled him in on what happened. Overseeing an extravagant wedding up in Seattle, my brother, the event planner, is likely calling to check up on me. Thank goodness, I didn't mention his name when I told

Brandon that Pops and Auntie Jo had a son. The phone rings and rings.

"Brandon, I have to take this. It's my boyfriend calling from out of town. He's been ... *think!* ... at some banking conference." My charade gives me little solace.

"Jeffrey?" Brandon's voice is as pinched as the expression on his face.

"Yes. He probably wants to know how I'm doing. I'm going to take the call in my room and then I'm going to get some rest."

"Fine," he huffs with resignation. "Let me know if you need anything."

I meet Brandon's piqued gaze and then walk away before tears betray me.

There's only one thing I need. Him. But he's not mine to be had.

The next day, while I'm ready and eager to go back to work to get my mind off Mama's murderer, Brandon insists I rest up for another twenty-four hours. Boss's orders. I can't say no and surrender.

It's like he's become a whole new person. He dotes on me. Gets me more chicken soup from Greenblatt's and checks in on me constantly. He even runs down to the newsstand on Sunset to buy me a dozen magazines so I won't get bored while he's studying his lines. I'm not used to the role reversal. I've always taken care of him, submitted to his every need. But now, he's taking care of me. I'm loving every minute—including having him wait outside the bathroom while I shower—but know it's not going to last. It's only a matter of time until Katrina shows up. I've refrained from asking Brandon about her whereabouts. Out of sight. Out of mind.

In the afternoon, we hang out together on the couch and binge on a *James Bond* marathon. Brandon has every 007 movie in his home library, and we start from the first, *Dr. No*, and then randomly watch Brandon's favorites.

Watching the movies with him is so much fun. We share a big bowl of popcorn—something he insists is a must. Brandon's totally into the flicks and he's surprisingly enlightening. Maybe my boss has lost part of his memory, but he's a walking encyclopedia when it comes to *James Bond*. He shares fascinating facts with me like Sean Connery wasn't the producers' first choice to play the iconic spy and that Cary Grant was up for the part.

"Does *James Bond* inspire you?" I ask, munching on some popcorn while he puts the next film into the DVD player. The remake of *Casino Royale*, one of the few *Bond* films I've never seen.

Brandon returns to the couch and snuggles up against me before hitting play. "Totally. Especially when I do my action scenes. I think—what would James Bond do?"

"What about your romantic scenes with Jewel?"

He tugs on his lower lip and then sensuously feeds me a popped kernel. "Yeah, sometimes. But lately, I've drawn from experience."

Katrina. My chest tightens, and I force the piece of popcorn past the lump in my throat.

"Who's your favorite James Bond?" I ask, referring to all the actors who've played the part though I know the answer.

"Hands down, Sean Connery."

"Mine too."

We end our conversation as the movie starts—as usual with an action-packed opening sequence that takes my breath away. In no time, I realize that the latest James Bond, Daniel Craig, is a close second to Sean Connery. While he's older, there's something so intense and sexy about him. And there's a vulnerability to him, too, that adds to his appeal. My breathing grows labored as I watch the sensuous shower scene between James and Vesper. It's one of the sexiest love scenes I've ever seen and makes me think of the shower I took with Brandon, both of us fully clothed. I know he's thinking about it too because I can feel heat radiating from his body. Maybe it inspired him, but I don't ask.

Our eyes stay glued to the big-screen TV as the movie comes to its gripping climax set in Venice. My heart hammers while tears fill my eyes. I'm overwhelmed with emotion.

"Oh, no!" I gasp as Vesper, trapped in an iron-frame lift, sinks deeper and deeper into a canal while James tries desperately to free her. "Please, Brandon, I can't watch this anymore."

Brandon turns to me, the expression on his face full of concern. "What's the matter?"

"I-I can't handle the drowning," I splutter, tears falling. "It reminds me of Mama."

"Shit." He immediately turns the TV off and brushes away my tears with a thumb. "I'm sorry, Zo. I should have been more sensitive."

My skin prickles at his tender touch. I quirk a little smile to let him know I'm okay. "It's not your fault. You didn't know how I'd react. And with Mama's murderer on my mind, I think I may be overreacting."

His eyes stay locked on mine. "You sure you're okay?"

I nod. "Yeah, I'm good. That was a great movie. I just wish Vesper didn't have to die like that."

"It's one of my favorites," concurs Brandon, his expression relaxing.

We share a brief moment of silence until I break it, never losing eye contact with him.

"I think you'd make a great James Bond, Brandon."

"You do?"

"Yeah, I do." The image of him in a tux on the night

of the Golden Globes flashes into my head. *Nobody does it better.* He'd bring a whole new level of sexiness to the role. Those mesmerizing violet eyes would make a box office killing.

"How's this for starters?"

"Go for it."

"The name's Bond. James Bond," he says with an utterly sexy and perfect British accent that makes me melt.

"That's brilliant!"

He smiles that million-dollar smile and renders me breathless. Then, before I can blink an eye, he scoops me into his arms and carries me away.

"What are you doing?" I laugh.

"Taking my Bond girl to bed," he answers, maintaining his alluring accent.

Me a Bond girl? I'm more like Miss Moneypenny. Goosebumps pop along my flesh while hot tingles dance between my legs. Taking his words at face value, I instantly fantasize Brandon as Bond seducing me. Transporting me to his bedroom and ravaging me on his bed. Devouring every ounce of me with his masculine prowess.

"It's almost midnight," he says. "You need to get a good night's sleep."

My fantasy is short-lived. But I relish being back in his arms. Over the past two days, he's been so kind, sweet, and funny. And so open.

"Why are you being so nice to me, Brandon?" I finally ask while he tucks me under the yummy covers. Maybe he has something up his sleeve. Or is putting on a good act. Or he's simply bi-polar.

"Because, believe it or not, I actually like you, Zoey. And care about you."

His words unnerve me. What does he mean? And does he really mean it? Before I can say a word, he hits me with an out of the blue question.

"Are you coming to my wedding?"

My heart clenches at the last word. Over the last forty-eight hours, I haven't given much thought to his upcoming marriage to Katrina.

"I wasn't invited," I mutter. The bitch didn't bother sending me an invitation though unknowingly she spared me the pain of opening it.

"I want you to attend." Brandon's voice is a soft command.

"As your assistant?"

"No, as my guest. I want you to be there for me."

My stomach churns at the mixed message his words send. I may wake up sick that morning. I can't bear the thought of watching Brandon and Katrina exchange their forever vows.

He flicks my nose. "Promise me you'll be there."

"Promise." My voice is so small I can barely hear myself. I refrain from asking him if my "boyfriend" can come. What's the point?

With a wistful smile, he turns off the light, and after he leaves, I close my eyes and enter the world of happily never after.

Chapter 3

Brandon

My life as Agent 007 is about to end. And it hasn't even begun.

I blink my eyes and take in my surroundings. I'm bound in a rope from head to toe and hooked to some kind of pulley.

Agent or rather Double Agent Katrina Moore is in my face. She fooled me. Her goddess-like beauty beguiled me. She knew I was a sucker for a beautiful woman. I should have known she was as fake as her silicone boobs. Fucking her should have been a clue too. After my showdown with her boss, the nefarious Piranha, she drugged me and tied me up and then took me to his headquarters, a decrepit warehouse in the middle of nowhere. Her feline eyes glow green with evil.

"Say goodbye to your life, James," she purrs. Wearing a skintight metallic jumpsuit and stilettos that match the color of her platinum hair, she leans into me, her jutting hipbones bruising me. The cloying smell of her cologne sickens me. I squirm as much as I can in the tight ropes.

She smiles wickedly. "I don't think your Olympic swimming skills are going to matter much."

My muscles tense. My eyes flit to the gigantic fifty-foot tank of water that's filled with hundreds of hungry piranhas. In minutes, I may be their new best friend, though it'll be a very short-lived relationship—no pun intended. Once I take the plunge and I'm bait, Katrina will rule Hollywood. Destroy every fish in the sea until she's controlling it all and sitting on billions while sending out her propaganda messages via infomercials that "Moore is More." Creating a society where everyone is clamoring to be a billionaire and forsaking every important value. Love. Family. Trust. Honor. Until everyone destroys each other, and she owns and controls every bank account in the world.

"Va te faire foutre," I say in French.

With a fling of her mane, Katrina lets out a haughty laugh. "Darling, you were always a cunning linguist. But your tongue was wasted on me."

Was it! She was the worst Bond girl I ever had. A frigid bitch.

She turns to her evil robotic cohort Scott, who is sitting behind a console with knobs and levers. "Scotty-

Botty, it's time to do the honors."

"Yes, ma-dame." His words are as mechanical as the automaton he is. It sickens me to think he was created by MI6 and was once my right hand man so to speak. It's too bad they could never figure out how to give him a heart. Katrina stole him from Her Majesty's Secret Service and programmed him to suit her needs. To destroy me.

The psycho bitch snaps her bony fingers twice. "Chop chop!"

The bot responds. He presses down on a massive lever, instantly hoisting me into the air. In seconds, my feet no longer touch the ground.

Katrina smirks. "Your career is about to reach new heights, James."

My eyes gaze up, then down. Already ten feet in the air, I'm headed to a dead end. It's time to kiss my illustrious career goodbye. I'll miss them all. M, Q, and especially Miss Moneypenny. I always had a thing for her. M's adorable secretary. She was basically my assistant too, taking care of my every need—from booking hotel rooms with my latest hookups to getting Q to supply me with the latest hi-tech weapons and cars. An image of her flashes in my mind. She's hardly like my Bond girls. They're supermodel perfect like Katrina. She, on the other hand, is a girl one might call ordinary. Slightly overweight… unstylish… pretty not beautiful. Yet, it's her big brown eyes, upturned nose, and kissable lips that fill my mind as death awaits me. My cock twitches beneath the ropes. Never having her is my only regret. I should have bent her over her desk and given her what she always wanted. At the thought of her ass in the air, my cock stiffens. At least, I'm going to die with a hard-on. As my inevitable fate awaits me, I feel stirred not shaken. If I survive this, I may change my martini of choice.

As I continue to ascend, Katrina keeps her eyes on my crotch. She scoffs. "There's nothing like being hung over a tank of hungry piranhas."

At least my cock will be hard to bite into. A small piece of solace.

"Do you like the view?"

"It's killer."

"Say goodbye, James."

Another voice...

"Say goodbye, Kuntrina!"

Miss Moneypenny! Sometimes you shouldn't be too careful for what you wish for. Dressed to kill in a little black dress that hugs all her luscious curves, she looks ravishing.

Katrina spins around. "What are you doing here, you sloth?"

Miss Moneypenny's eyes clash with Katrina's. "Not wasting my time talking to you."

"I don't waste *my* time talking to peons."

"You're going to be sorry you said that." On her

next breath, Miss Moneypenny charges at Katrina, tackling and knocking her to the ground. She tears at her metallic jumpsuit.

"You bitch! You're ruining my outfit! It's Versace! You're going to pay a pretty penny to replace it!"

"I'm not even going to take it to a tailor," retorts Moneypenny, straddling Katrina and holding her down while she screams and writhes.

My eyes stay riveted on her full, heart-shape arse, and I have the burning desire to spread those huggable cheeks apart. Where there's a will, there's a way, M always preached. Scott the Bot meanwhile hoists me higher. I'm now about twenty-five feet in the air. In a few minutes, I'm going to be fish food.

Katrina and Moneypenny continue to go at each other madly, exchanging every expletive in the dictionary. They roll about on the floor. Hissing. Gnawing. Scratching. Fisting. Clumps of hair go flying. It looks like Katrina has the upper hand, stabbing her adversary with the spiky heel of her killer stiletto. Again and again and again.

"Die, you fat bitch!" she screams.

"You die first!" rasps back Moneypenny after another blow. To my utter astonishment, she reaches into her impressive cleavage and yanks out a shiny six-inch knife. She holds it over Katrina. Katrina's eyes flicker with terror.

"Don't you dare kill me!" she shrieks. "I'll give you

anything you want! All the money in the world!"

Moneypenny slowly lowers the knife. "There's only one thing I want, and it's not your money. And besides, my name comes with it."

The knife is millimeters from Katrina. Her face is frozen with fear. Moneypenny holds her fierce in her gaze.

"Rot in hell, bitch!"

"Noooooo!"

Katrina's mouth never closes as Moneypenny plunges the blade into her chest. *Splat!* My nemesis lets out a deep groan as her right breast deflates and jelled liquid seeps out from the three-inch tear in her jumpsuit.

"Ha! I always new they were fake!" Moneypenny smiles with smug victory and then looks up at me. "Hang on, James!"

My eyes stay on her as she dashes over to the pulley that's hoisting me. With a whoosh, she slices the cord like a swashbuckler. I fall thirty feet to the ground, but it's a hell of a lot better than falling into a tank full of man-eating piranhas. I've always preferred hard surfaces.

"James, are you okay?" asks a concerned Moneypenny, squatting down beside me. Wasting no time, she cuts though the binding rope and sets me free.

Slowly, I sit up, facing her. I give her nose an affectionate flick. "I like a girl with a knife."

She grins. But not for long. The smile on her face falls off and her eyes grow wide with terror. "James, watch out!"

I spin around like a top. Fuck. Scott the Bot, who's programmed to kill me, is coming at me at breakneck speed.

"Die, Bond." Two monotone syllables. A lethal laser shoots out of one arm, but I move out of harm's way just in the nick of time. On my next breath, I reach into the breast pocket of my tuxedo and pull out my Beretta. I aim it and fire. *Bang!* I get the automaton right between the eyes, leaving a bullet-sized hole. And then I fire the gun two more times, aiming for his eyes. *Bang! Bang!* Double bullseye! His eyes pop out of their sockets, hanging on by mere springs. Deprogrammed, the bot spins around in crazy circles until he collapses onto the floor with a clang.

I rotate on my arse again and face Moneypenny. A seductive smile lights up her face. "And I like a man with a gun."

"Miss Moneypenny—"

"My name is Zoey."

"Zoey." I love the way her name rolls off my tongue. All these years together and I never knew her first name. It's as beautiful as she is. My cock rises to full attention.

Then, her face grows serious again. "Oh, James. If you died, I'd—"

Tilting up her chin, I silence her with a fierce kiss. She melts into me. It's as if her soft lips have always belonged on mine. Her tongue finds my tongue and they dance together, swirling and twirling, as if they've done this forever. She fists my hair, and her supple breasts press against my chest. I can feel her nipples harden like bullets beneath the fabric of my tux. She moans into my mouth. I want to fuck her more than I want to serve Her Majesty. I want her to be mine. She *will* be mine. I've never failed at a mission.

I break the kiss and reach for a handful of the rope.

"James, what are you doing?"

"I'm going to properly thank you for saving my life." Q always told me actions speak louder than words. On my next heated breath, I twist the rope around her wrists, binding them together, and then attach them to a floor-to-ceiling metal pipe. Seeing her tied up like this makes my cock crazy with want. Without wasting a second, I scrunch up her little dress to her hips and rip off her scanty lace panties. I take whiff before tossing them. It's like I've inhaled a drug. I can't wait to get more. Sitting back on my calves, I spread her legs and bury my head between her thighs. It's the most beautiful sight I've ever seen. Her pussy so pink and glistening. I can't wait to taste her. My talented tongue darts out of my hungry mouth and dips into her carnal lips. Jesus. She's more delicious than I even imagined. I greedily lick and flick her sweet slickness.

Arching, she moans. "Oh, Sir James."

Her calling me sir only gets me more excited. None of my Bond girls ever called me that though I was knighted. Such respect and submission.

"How does it feel, Zoey?"

"Oh, James, I can't find the words."

"Well, then, let me try to enlarge your vocabulary." My tongue moves to her clit. It licks and flicks until I feel a hard throbbing nub at the tip. Her breathing grows harsh. A symphony of pants and moans plays in my ears.

"Now, tell me, Zoey. How does that feel?"

"Oh please don't stop! I need more!"

I love that she's begging for me. And so polite. "Zoey, I need more specific words." I nip her.

She gasps. "So good."

"Please say: 'So good, sir.'"

She does as asked and I go back to my ministrations, loving every minute of her tantalizing pussy and responsive clit. She's dripping with want. I plunge a finger into her slit and pump her. God, she's so wet and tight. I can't wait to fuck her.

Her breathing grows more ragged. She begins to writhe, trying desperately to free herself from the pole. The moans become whimpers. And the whimpers become sobs. I love a damsel in distress.

"What do you want, Zoey?"

"I want to come, sir! Please!"

"You'll come when I say you can. From now on, you're mine. Only mine. Say it—"

"I'm yours. Only yours!"

"I own your orgasms, do you understand?"

She nods feverishly.

"Zoey, I need words."

"Yes, I understand."

The passion in her voice—and her submission—are all I need. I give her pussy a nice slap, and as she yelps, I kiss her clit and suck away the sting.

"Oh, James!"

"Come for me, Zoey. Don't hold back." I press my lips back on her divine pussy, and with the next flick of my tongue, she explodes in my face with a gush of wetness. Best of all, she screams my name. The way it's spoken stirs me to the core. It's time for her to get to know my other big gun.

"Lie down. Hands above your head. Then bend your knees and spread them wide."

Silently, she does as told, and at the sight of her, I feel my cock swell, as if bigger is possible. She's truly exceptional. Her pussy so ready, her nub a crimson rosebud and the delicate wet petals of her cleft an exquisite shade of pink. Her thighs quiver.

Our eyes connect.

"James, you've never even taken me to dinner."

"No, I've never taken you to dinner looking like

this. Let me give you something to digest."

On my knees between her legs, I undo the clasp of my pants and zip down my fly. My hard as a rock cock springs out like a jack in the box. Her jaw drops to her chest and she gasps.

I don't think I've ever had such a powerful erection. It curls to my navel. There's even a bead of pre-cum on the tip. "Do I come up to your expectations?"

"Oh, James, so beyond! Please, James, I need you inside me!"

"My dear, I'm going to fuck you until you detonate. Blow you up into a million little pieces. I'm going to make you come so loud, so hard you're going to scare the fish."

"Oh James, take me. You can have me any time. Anywhere. Whatever is left of me, whatever I am, I'm yours!"

She has no idea. I lean into her, placing one hand on the cold cement to anchor myself, and the other around my enormous shaft. I rub it along her soaked folds and then I put it at her entrance. Inch by thick inch, I glide it inside her until I hit the warm, wet velvet of her womb. She clenches around me. And then I hear another scream.

"I'm not done with you, James."

The voice is a hoarse, deranged whisper, but I'd recognize it anywhere. Katrina! She's alive! Still inside Zoey, I crank my neck and her venomous eyes collide with mine. Zoey's knife is in her hands. Before I can blink, a white-hot pain sears me…

Fade to black.

At the sound of my alarm, I bolt up in my bed. It takes me a moment to realize that I'm back to being me. And that I'm alive. I've got a giant boner and I'm shaking like a leaf. The blurred line between reality and fantasy frightens me. My dream's as vivid as the morning light. I try to make sense of it.

It's sending me a message. About my need for dominance. And my need for my assistant. Zoey's under my skin and in my bloodstream. She lives in my soul and makes me feel whole.

But my gut tells me this dream is an ominous warning. An omen. A chill runs through me from my head to my toes. Things are so goddamn complicated. My fucking life is totally out of control.

Chapter 4

Zoey

The next day, I'm feeling a lot stronger physically, so Brandon lets me spend more time up and about. I spend most of my time helping him with some lines and, like it or not, responding to the never-ending tweets about the status of Bratrina. He seems a little on edge. When I ask him why, he tells me he's got a lot on his mind and didn't sleep well. That makes two of us. Visions of Donatelli and my mother's brutal death haunted me as did Brandon's pending marriage to Katrina.

In the late afternoon, he orders me to put my laptop away and we snuggle on the couch to watch another rough-cut of an upcoming *Kurt Kussler* episode. Both of us relax. Halfway through it, my phone rings. Brandon puts the show on pause while I answer it.

It's Pops! He's back in town and wants to come

over. He's eager to talk to me.

Forty-five minutes later, he's at the house. I hug him at the front door.

"Oh, Pops! I'm so glad you're here."

"How are you doing, Babycakes?"

I smile and usher him in. "I'm doing better."

"I'm taking good care of her, Detective." Widening my smile, I cast my eyes at Brandon who's come to join us. "I'm about to order in some sandwiches from Greenblatt's. Would you like one?"

"Thanks, but no thanks. I won't be staying long. The missus wants me home for dinner. Boss's orders."

Brandon and I both laugh. "What about a beer then?" he asks.

Pops's eyes light up. "Now, that I'll take."

"Me too," I chime in.

Brandon shoots me a dirty look and waggles a reprimanding finger. "Uh-uh-uh. No beer for you. You can't have any alcohol while you're on your meds. *Your* boss's orders. Understood?"

I make a face. "Yes, sir." Brandon's face lights up at the last word.

While Brandon goes to the kitchen to get the beers, Pops shrugs off his trench coat and makes himself at home, taking a seat in one of Brandon's oversized chairs. I curl up on the couch. Someone who wastes no time, Pops gets right into it.

"So Babycakes, tell me again what happened."

I launch into my story and tell him how I'm sure I saw Brandon's manager Scott having coffee with Mama's murderer. "Pops, I'm more than a hundred percent sure it was him. You know I'd never forget his face. Yeah, he looked older, but it was him. I'm absolutely positive."

"I believe you, Babycakes. The problem is we can't find any witnesses who saw two men who matched those descriptions. The Farmer's Market is a big open space with diverse locals and tourists who come and go. My team's spoken to all the vendors, and at best, they've gotten something like, 'That sounds like a lot of people who stop by.'"

"Maybe they caught something on a surveillance camera," I offer. Between growing up with Pops and watching a lot of *Kurt Kussler*, I could practically be a detective myself.

Pops glumly shakes his head. "I wish. Unfortunately, The Farmer's Market doesn't have a surveillance system."

My heart sinks. We're still at square one. Brandon returns with two Heinekens and a Diet Coke for me. *Mr. Thoughtful.*

"Help yourselves," he says, setting the bottles on the coffee table. Snatching a beer, he lowers himself on the couch next to me. His thigh brushes against mine and I can feel his warmth.

"Why is Scott lying?" I throw the question out to

both Pops and Brandon after taking a swig of my soda. "Pops, you should make him take a lie detector test."

"They're unreliable." He grabs a beer and takes several gulps.

Brandon plays devil's advocate. "What makes you think he's lying?"

What! He doesn't believe me now? My face scrunches with anger and my voice rises an octave. "Because he is! He's a total slimebucket. I wouldn't believe a word that man said. I bet he even told you he's the one who found you unconscious on the day of your accident."

Setting his beer bottle back down on the table, Brandon blinks several times the way he does whenever he's having a recall moment. He looks flustered… unsure. "He did. While I was in the hospital, he said he called it in. Saved my ass."

My stomach twists. I didn't really mean what I said. A cocktail of shock and rage shoots through me. "Fucking liar! Newsflash: *I'm* the one who found you and called 911." *The one who held you, prayed for you, kissed…* I banish the memory of that day before tears betray me.

Pops corroborates what I've said. "It's true. Zoey did. We still have the dispatcher's recording."

Brandon is stunned into silence. Finally, in a soft voice, he says, "Zoey, why didn't you tell me?"

My voice softens too. "I thought you knew."

"I'm sorry, Zo." He brushes his hand along my jawline. His tender touch sets me on fire. I feel myself flushing with tingles all over. Wondering if Pops notices, I glance his way. His brows are furrowed, his lips pressed together, and he's rubbing a thumb across his dimpled chin. I know that expression. I've seen it a zillion times before. He's onto something.

"Pops, what are you thinking?"

He lowers his hand, but his brows remain knitted. "If Scott Turner is lying, that changes everything."

"What do you mean?"

"Babycakes, tell me again the conversation you overheard. Word for word."

Thanks to my eidetic memory, I recite it as if I've just heard it, making use of my acting skills to imitate their voices. "The man who shot Mama shouted, 'You fucked up once. Don't do it again.' And then Scott nervously replied, 'Okay, okay, I'll take care of it.'"

Almost instantly, I gasp and clasp my hand to my mouth. I construe their exchange in a whole new way. "Pops, do you think they were referring to Brandon's hit and run?"

Pops looks at me with intensity. "Possibly. The two of them may have something to do with it. I have a hunch someone's trying to knock off Brandon. And there could be a connection between the accident and your mother's murder."

Brandon and I both quietly digest Pops's words.

Brandon breaks the silence. "Detective, what's the next step?"

"I want Zoey to come into headquarters tomorrow and talk to our sketch artist. We need to find out who this man is."

"I'll bring her. I don't want her driving yet, especially downtown."

Pops smiles warmly. "Thanks. Afterward, I'm going to talk to Scott. Check out his cell phone as well as his alibi and do some digging. Maybe we can dredge up something that ties everything together. Maybe there's even a connection to Kremins."

"Kremins?" asks Brandon, puzzled.

Pops fills Brandon in. Conrad Kremins was the man who was shot along with Mama. What Pops learned in the investigation of their murders was that he was a sleazy sex club operator who had a lot of enemies and was in major debt. My mother's bullet was probably meant for him.

A pang of sadness assaults me at the thought of her senseless murder before giving way to a burst of optimism and excitement. Pops is going to find the evil man who did this to her! And uncover the cruel person who ran Brandon over and left him for dead. I just know it.

Setting my soda down, I leap up from the couch and give my father another big hug. "Oh, Pops, you're the best!"

He laughs his hearty laugh. "We're going to solve this mystery once and for all." He turns to Brandon and, with a wink, does his best Kurt Kussler imitation: "Get it. Got it? ..."

"Good," chimes in Brandon, smiling brightly. He really seems to like my dad.

"One last thing. Brandon, do you have a body-guard?"

Brandon screws up his face. "No way. I'm an action hero. I can take care of myself. And I don't like people following me around."

Pops twists his mouth. "I seriously think you should have one. Your life may be in jeopardy."

Brandon polishes off his beer. "I'll think about it."

Knowing my headstrong boss, I doubt he'll acqui-esce. Despite the megastar he is, he's never traveled with an entourage except on very special occasions like award shows.

Pops presses his lips thin. My perceptive father already knows it's futile. "Well then, until you decide, I'm going to set up twenty-four hour police surveillance outside your house. I can't have my daughter in danger either."

Brandon twitches a half-smile. "That's a good idea." He pauses, casting his eyes my way. "And I'm going to make sure nothing happens to her. Zoey means a lot to me."

At his unexpected words, I feel myself flushing and

once again try to process what he just said.

"I appreciate that, Brandon. She means a lot to me too," Pops says before glancing down at his battered watch. "Gotta go. The missus is waiting for me. Oh, and by the way, she can't thank you enough for those signed DVDs. She displays the box on our fireplace mantle like it's some rare piece of art."

Brandon's megawatt smile widens. God, he's so gorgeous when he smiles. "Glad to hear that. Can you hang out for a minute?"

"Sure," says Pops as Brandon jogs out of the room. He returns in no time, holding what looks to be a glossy photo. Sure enough, it's a miniature version of the shattered *Kurt Kussler* poster I still have propped up against a wall in my bedroom. He hands it to Pops.

"I've already signed it."

"Holy baloney! She's going to love this!"

Brandon is beaming like a proud boy scout. "And tell her, she can drop by the set anytime she wants. Just have her call Zoey to arrange for a pass to get onto the lot." He shoots me a saucy wink.

Clenching my teeth, I shoot him back a look that says "screw you, asshole." He always has to one up me with my father, making me look like the bad guy. I try to keep my cool, but Brandon's flirtatious, cocky grin makes it difficult.

"Sure. No problem." A retaliatory smirk and then I pause. "Brandon, I'm going to walk my father to his car, if that's okay with you. I think I can handle it."

Brandon stands and shakes my father's hand. "Take good care of her, Detective. I need her around. We'll see you tomorrow."

The late January night air is crisp and refreshing. The lit up LA skyline is basked in moonlight. It feels good to be outside having been cooped up in Brandon's house for almost two days though I shouldn't be complaining. I've been treated like a queen, waited and doted on by the King of Good Looking. I walk Pops to his car, which is parked in the driveway. He buckles up his rumpled trench coat while I lift up the wide collar.

"Pops, you really should get a new coat. It's time."

"Yeah, yeah, I know. That's what your mother says too. But I like this one."

I giggle. You can't change Pops. He digs his hand into a pocket and retrieves his car keys. He could use a new car too, but knowing Pops, he'll be buried in the one he's driving. A 1985 Chevy Impala that he's had since his first day on the force.

Catching me distracted, he tilts up my chin with the thumb of his other hand.

"Babycakes, you like him."

I laugh lightly. Nervously "He's my boss. He's an asshole most of the time."

He tilts my chin higher "You more than like him. You're in love with him."

A sudden chill sweeps over me. My heart stutters. "What makes you say that, Pops?"

"I'm a detective. I may not read big books with fancy words, but I read body language."

My father can read people like an encyclopedia. That's what makes him so good at his job. My chest tightens, my throat constricts, and my heart speeds up. I let him continue because I'm speechless.

"It's the little things. The way you look at him. Hang on to his every word. The tilt of your head. Those little eye tics. The way you let him touch you."

Tears cluster in my eyes. My voice is a rasp. "It's that obvious?"

He brushes away a rebel tear that's fallen. "Yupparoo." Before I can bemoan my fate, he adds, "And he's in love with you."

My heart skips a loud beat. That can't be! I'm just his overweight, lowly assistant. "Pops, what are you talking about?"

"Trust me, I can tell. He can't take his eyes off you. I saw the way those purple orbs tenderly held you when he found out you called 911. And how his hand brushed along your jaw. Only a man in love would do that."

Pops's heartfelt words are almost like poetry. Powerful emotions pull my chest apart. Like a tug of war. There is so much of me that wants to believe what my father just said, but doubt yanks at my heartstrings.

"Pops, he's in love with Katrina. He just doesn't remember. I'm not even his type."

Moving both hands to my shoulders, Pops holds my teary gaze in his loving gray eyes. "Babycakes, you may not be his type, but you're his preference. Trust me, I've seen that Katrina and she doesn't hold a candle to you."

I warm at Pops's compliment, but it doesn't change reality. I remind him they're getting married on national TV in May.

Unfazed, Pops smiles. "A lot can change in a couple of months." He unlocks the car door and then swings it open. Before sliding into the beat up vehicle, he slaps a kiss on my forehead.

"Life's not a done deal. One kiss… one night… one memory… can change everything. See you two kids tomorrow."

He scoots into the car, turns on the cranky ignition, and then pulls out of the driveway. I hug myself to keep warm as he disappears into the night.

Chapter 5

Zoey

"Holy mother of Jesus! Is that who I think it is?" gasps Alma Lopez, who's co-manning the front desk at my father's busy downtown precinct.

I can't help smiling. "Yes, Alma. Meet my boss, Brandon Taylor."

Looking like she may faint, the flustered officer's breathing grows shallow as she begins to fan herself. *"Dios mío!"*

"I'd be honored to take a photo with you before I leave," says Brandon, acting every bit the star he is. "You can post it on Instagram or Facebook or wherever you want."

My eyes stay on Brandon while my smile grows bigger. I just love the way he gives back to his adoring fans. So willingly and unabashedly. So many stars don't. I remember once when I was thirteen with a plaster cast on my arm (a stupid rollerblading accident), I encountered a famous star (sorry, no names) who I adored in a restaurant and built up the courage to ask him to sign the cast. The asshole refused. "Excuse me. I'd like to enjoy my lunch," he said coldly and dismissively shooed me away. He made me feel like I was three feet tall. Total humiliation!

More and more people recognize Brandon while Alma calls my father. In no time, he's mobbed. It's almost a sitcom. Even the drunk homeless guy recognizes him and begs him to sign his tattered blanket. Brandon is cordial to everyone, regardless of race, background, or creed. With a big smile, he poses for one photo after another and signs autographs for everyone on everything—from body parts and outerwear to subpoenas and parole papers.

A familiar voice grabs my attention. Pops. Munching on a sandwich, he lumbers through the security door. He grins at the sight of Brandon's fandom.

"C'mon, Babycakes. Brenda, our sketch artist, is eager to meet with you."

I tug at Brandon's non-stop autographing arm. He turns to me and I'm seriously in awe of how hot damn gorgeous he is even under unflattering florescent lighting. My heart thuds.

"I'm going with Pops to meet with the sketch artist."

"Want me to come with you?" he asks while signing someone's police report.

Pops answers before I can. "It's better if they're one on one." And then he grins. "Besides you have your work cut out for you."

"It's all in the line of duty," retorts Brandon with a line that's straight out of a *Kurt Kussler* episode.

After exchanging a smile with my busy superstar boss, I follow Pops through the door to a small, windowless room at the end of a long, bustling hallway. An attractive, casually dressed forty-something woman with a coil of copper curls is seated at a table. She smiles at me warmly.

"Hi, I'm Brenda"

I glance at her badge. Her full name: Brenda McKay. Her sparkling hazel eyes meet mine.

"We're going to work together to figure out who this asshole is."

I like her... her choice of words... her fuck-the-bastard mentality.

"I'm ready," I say, taking a seat across from her. In addition to her laptop and a tablet, numerous binders are scattered on the surface of the table. The memory of talking to a sketch artist right after Mama's shooting comes back to me as if it were only yesterday. The binders are filled with reference images that will help me pinpoint the features of the man I saw with Scott and help Brenda build her facial composite.

"Babycakes, I'll be back shortly," says Pops. "Don't

hold back. Brenda is top notch." My eyes follow him out the door.

Brenda turns her laptop so that the screen faces me. I watch as she lays a sheet of paper over the tablet.

"Don't you have a sketch pad?" I ask, remembering how fascinated I was by the sketch artist I met with when I was five-years old.

"You're looking at it," she says, adjusting the sheet of paper. "We're going to do this digitally. While I draw on my tablet, you'll be able to see the image on the laptop screen and let me know if I need to make adjustments."

"Cool!" Just like on *Kurt Kussler!* LAPD has joined the twenty-first century.

Brenda begins her interrogation. Not only do criminal sketch artists need to have drawing skills, but they also need people and listening skills.

"So, Zoey, tell me about the man you saw. What did he look like?" Brenda's voice is warm and immediately puts me at ease.

With my eidetic memory, I picture him clearly in my mind's eye. "He had a broad, pockmarked face with a squashed nose. Oh, and a really thick neck."

As I talk, Brenda sketches, and an outline of the suspect's face materializes on my computer screen.

"Like this?" she asks.

"Kind of. His face was squarer and his nose more spread out. Like it's been broken a few times." I flip through one of the reference books to show her what I mean. She modifies the sketch.

"Yes! Like that!" Excitement colors my voice.

"Tell me about his eyes."

"They were dark and beady. Very close together."

"And his brows?"

"Dark and bushy. Very close to his eyes."

"Did they cross the bridge of his nose?"

"Yes. They met in the middle."

"And what about his hair?"

"Reddish brown. Very short. Almost a buzz." I flip through another notebook until I find an almost identical hairline.

"And his mouth?"

"Like a pair of sausages."

My eyes grow as wide as saucers as I watch the face take shape. And then as Brenda fills in the lips, I gasp at the image on the laptop screen.

"Oh my God! That's him!"

"Are you sure, Zoey?"

"I'm one hundred percent positive."

"Let me call your father." My eyes stay on the composite while she uses the tabletop phone to summon Pops. Every nerve in my body is buzzing with anticipation.

Two minutes later, Pops rejoins us. A thick accordion folder is in his hand. It's marked: Case #1567: Angela Hart. My mother's file. It's now considered a cold case though Pops has never stopped searching for Mama's murderer. He plops down on the chair next to mine and sets the file down next to the laptop. Reaching inside it, he withdraws a sheet of paper and lays it flat on the table. I recognize it immediately. It's the police sketch of the man who fired a gun at me twenty years ago. My eyes bounce from it to the computer screen with the new sketch and then flick to my father.

"Pops, they're one and the same!" Even though the man I just described is substantially heavier and now has a receding hairline and facial lines that show his age, they are undoubtedly the same person. The same ugly monster. My heart is racing.

"Brenda, can you run your new sketch through our data base and see if we can get a match?"

"Absolutely."

With baited breath, I wait for the results. This is something that wasn't possible to do twenty years ago. Computer technology has allowed for so many breakthroughs in criminology.

In a matter of seconds, a mug shot appears on the screen next to the sketch. My heart skips a beat.

"Pops! That's him! The man I saw with Scott! Mama's murderer!"

Wordlessly, Pops presses a couple of keys on the laptop keyboard. In a few rapid heartbeats, the suspect's name pops up.

Pops reads it aloud.

"Frank Donatelli. Age 51."

Hastily, he puts the phone on speaker and punches a four-digit extension.

"Mancuso," booms a deep voice on the first ring.

"It's Pete. I'm with Brenda." Pops's voice is urgent. "Get me everything you can on Frank Donatelli. I need it NOW!"

"On it." The call ends.

Five minutes later, Lieutenant Mancuso, one of Pops's favorite and most reliable officers on the force, joins us, with a printout in his hand. He hands it to Pops. Pops slips his reading glasses that are on top of his head over the bridge of his nose. With lips pressed tight, he reads the material.

"Fuck."

"What, Pops?"

"Donatelli is a loan shark who works for the Mob. He's known as 'The Finger'—for both his fuck-you attitude and his trigger-happy skills."

"You should be able to find him."

"Babycakes, it's not that easy. He's a ghost."

"What do you mean?"

"He's invisible. Off the grid. No address. No social security number. Uses fake identities and only burner phones. In other words, he's untraceable."

My heart sinks to my stomach. If Pops doesn't think he can find him, no one can.

"What's the next step?" I ask my father, my voice

thick with disappointment.

"We're going to circulate his photo, issue a warrant for his arrest, and maybe bring in the FBI." He pauses. "And have someone on the force keep an eye on Scott. They may have contact again."

"Do you still think his meeting with Scott had something to do with Brandon?"

Pops rubs his dimpled chin. "Not sure yet. I've been thinking about it. Maybe it has something to do with you."

I inwardly shudder. "Pops, I'm positive he didn't recognize me." While I've never lost all my baby fat, I no longer look like the chubby, pigtailed little girl who witnessed her mother's murder. "And besides he has no clue about my identity or whereabouts."

The latter is true because the police kept my name out of the press to protect me. Frustrated, Pops rakes his stubby fingers through his full head of slate hair. His face is pinched.

"Has Scott ever threatened you?"

"Pops, he threatened to fire me, but he's never threatened my life." Yet, I wonder—does despicable Scott despise me enough to want to kill me? Is that motive enough?

"Does he perceive you as a threat?"

I answer Pops honestly. "Somewhat. He doesn't like my relationship with Brandon, but truthfully, I don't think it would drive him to kill me."

"Babycakes, at this point, we can't rule anything out. I've seen people kill for no reason at all." He turns to Mancuso. "Mancuso, do a thorough investigation of Brandon Taylor's manager, Scott Turner, and get me everything you have on him as quickly as you can."

"Will do boss. I'll get on it right away," the uniformed officer replies, already out the door.

Pops returns his attention to the computer, and with a couple clicks of the mouse, prints out Donatelli's image. "Brenda, would you do me a favor and grab the printout."

"Sure," she says, swiveling her chair to retrieve the photo that's spewing out of the printer behind her. She faces front again and hands it to Pops.

"Thanks," says Pops, carefully slipping the photo into Mama's case folder. "And thanks for working with Zoey and doing a stellar job."

Brenda smiles proudly. "My pleasure. I hope you nail the bastard."

Rising with the folder in his hand, Pops takes a deep breath. "Me too."

I can read him like a book and detect a shadow of doubt.

He gives me an affectionate noogie. "C'mon, Babycakes. I'll walk you back to the front desk." I stand, and he wraps a comforting arm around my shoulders.

When we return to the front desk area, there's a line out the door to get Brandon's autograph or take a photo with him. Alma is shouting out for people to behave themselves. Despite my glum mood, I can't help smiling.

"Sorry, guys. Last autograph," I hear him say when he catches sight of me. Despite the moans and groans of the disappointed bystanders, all eager to have a moment of glory with America's favorite action hero, he struts over to Pops and me.

"How did it go?"

"Pretty good," I say with a heavy heart.

"What do you mean?"

Pops chimes in. "We've identified the man who murdered Zoey's mother. But it's gong to be difficult to nail him." He slips his hand into the thick folder and shows Brandon the photo of Frank Donatelli.

All blood drains from Brandon's face. His eyes almost pop out of their sockets. He looks as if he's just seen a ghost.

"Holy fuck! This can't be!"

"What, Brandon?" I ask, never seeing him like this before.

"It's him! The bastard who rammed into my parents' car and killed them."

My jaw drops and I've never seen Pops look so surprised. "Frank Donatelli?"

"No. Arthur Fratianne. But I swear on my life, it's the same bastard."

Pops slips the photo back into the file. His face

darkens. "Brandon, we now have a new suspect in your hit and run."

My eyes dart from Brandon to Pops and then back to Brandon.

An unprecedented blanket of rage falls over his beautiful face. His violet eyes narrow into switchblades. His nostrils flare while his chest rises and falls.

"I want the motherfucker dead."

Chapter 6

Brandon

If yesterday started with a bolt of lightning—I'm still not over the fact that Zoey's mother's killer is the bastard responsible for my parents' demise and neither is she—today starts with a clap of thunder.

Hurricane Katrina. Clutching Gucci, clad in his latest pink designer outfit and matching bow, she storms into the living room where Zoey and I are eating breakfast on the couch and dissecting all the mind-boggling motives behind our intertwined cases. A uniformed livery trails her, wheeling a massive pink suitcase.

"What the hell is *she* doing here?" she shrieks, shooting eye daggers at Zoey and cutting our conversation short.

"I had Zoey stay over because of her concussion."

"You mean that stupid little bump on her head you

blew me off for?" Adjusting her gazillion dollar fur coat, she looks at me harshly. "You owe me a dinner."

"We can go to the Polo Lounge tonight." I turn to Zoey. "Zoey, can you please make us a res—"

Katrina cuts me off. "It's too late. I'm off to New York for Fashion Week. I'm taping segments there for my series."

Great. A week away from her! I inwardly sigh with relief. I need the time to think things through. I still don't feel a thing for her in my heart or my soul. Nor can my brain remember a damn thing about our past. And she does nothing to arouse my cock. The only thing she gets up is my blood pressure.

My relief is short-lived. Not only does the obnoxious mutt growl at me, but Katrina also throws me a curve ball.

"And, darling, you're going to meet me there next Thursday. Scott booked *The Letterman Show* for us."

What the fuck! This is all news to me. Why didn't Scott tell me? Or even Zoey? I ask my fiancée why I'm just learning this. She tells me it happened last minute—on her way over here.

"I don't think I can make it. I'm shooting all next week." *And I don't want to leave Zoey alone.*

"Make it work. And be sure to bring Gucci with you."

I deconstruct her words. "What are you saying?"

"I'm leaving Gucci with you. As much as I would

love to take him with me, it's way too cold in New York for my little boy to be running around from show to show. And I just haven't had the time to buy him a winter coat and booties." She turns to the stoic livery. "I've packed all his LA outfits, his favorite toys, and his special dietary needs. He prefers home-cooked meals and is especially fond of poached eggs with smoked salmon."

"What about his bed?" I stammer.

"Darling, Gucci only sleeps in real beds. So, he'll be sleeping with you. Get used to it." She smiles smugly while the menacing dog growls at me again.

"Oh, and by the way, while I'm here, can I please have my birthday present? Scott told me you bought me a bauble."

Balls. I totally forgot about it. And have no idea what Zoey purchased with my credit card. Hopefully, it's in her car, which is still parked at The Farmer's Market.

Zoey covers for me. "Katrina, it hasn't arrived yet. Brandon special ordered something for you online from Tiffany's. It should be here any day." She pauses, taking a long breath. "It's beautiful."

God, I love my assistant! She's the one who deserves something special from Tiffany's.

Katrina flashes a smile before her catty green eyes narrow. "Follow up on it, Zoey. And Brandon, be sure to bring whatever it is to New York. I want to show it off on *Letterman*."

"I will," I mutter, making a mental note to have Zoey arrange for a PA from the show to pick up her car later today. Taking her back to The Farmer's Market so soon might upset her. I'm also going to call Scott and tell him to cancel my appearance. If Katrina wants to go on *Letterman* and tell the world about our relationship—or lack of one—fine. I'll just FedEx the bauble to her.

Katrina cuts into my thoughts. "Now, Brandy-Poo, take Gucci from me."

Is she kidding? The last thing I want to do is hold that nasty, finger-biting beast. Snarling, it bears those tiny razor-sharp teeth and eyes me hungrily. The painful memory of being bit on the toe by the vicious canine flashes into my head.

"Um, uh…" This is pathetic. Seriously? Me, Kurt Kussler, TV's most fearless action hero, is afraid of an itsy bitsy, teeny-weeny little dog.

Thank God, Zoey steps in. "I'll take him." Standing up, she gathers the little white fur ball from Katrina and holds him in her arms. Wagging his tail, the dog seems to like her.

"Very well. And Zoey, since you're the live-in maid around this place, don't forget to walk him three times a day. His walking schedule is in the suitcase along with his pooper scooper and leash." Katrina eyes Zoey with scorn. "I just hope with your condition and weight, you can keep up with him."

I mentally growl at my fiancée. It's time for her to stop insulting my priceless assistant. "Katrina, please apologize to Zoey. There was no need to say that."

Katrina shoots me a dirty look before my assistant responds.

"Katrina, I don't need your apology. And just FYI, I'm in great shape."

I can confirm that. Every luscious curve of her body drives me crazy with desire. And it's not just her body. Or her adorable face. Over the last forty-eight hours, I've grown connected to her in ways I never imagined. And it's not just because her mother's murder and my hit and run may be connected. Or the fact that she saved my life. It's more than that. She makes me laugh and lets me be myself. I feel comfortable opening up to her and she listens. And I love how she believes in me despite my own insecurities. Maybe my amnesia has released feelings I previously suppressed.

Katrina rolls her eyes and then kisses Gucci on the head. "Be a good boy for Mommy."

Afterward, she gives me a peck on my cheek. "Goodbye, darling, I've got a plane to catch. See you on Thursday night."

"Right." *Wrong.*

She snaps her fingers at the livery guy. "Chop chop. We don't want to be late." She parades out of my living room with the chauffeur trailing behind her.

"Zoey, what are we going to do with this beast?" I ask after I hear their car pull away.

"We're going to take care of him." Smiling, she lifts the mutt up to her face. "Hi, sweetie pie. Say hello to your *new* mommy."

To my astonishment, the fluffy little dog wags his tail again and laps her face.

"He really likes you."

Zoey giggles as Gucci continues to lavish her with kisses. I have to admit…it's so damn cute.

"Mr. Taylor, if you don't already know, I'm very likeable."

And very kissable.

Maybe dog sitting will be fun. Just the thing we need to get our minds off Frank fucking Donatelli. And my mind off Katrina.

Gucci follows Zoey everywhere. The little white dog is a boundless bundle of energy and spins circles around the house. At noon, before I head over to the set, Zoey tells me she's going to walk him.

"Are you going to put on one of his outfits?"

"No way. Gucci's a boy and all his outfits are pink. Katrina has him totally confused. Poor thing."

I laugh. My connection to my loveable assistant can't be denied and grows closer by the minute. She's like my soul mate. We both come from loving, hard-working middle-class families, have suffered personal tragedies that are strangely related, and share a sense of humor. Plus, a passion for James Bond. There's nothing I have in common with spoiled "It girl" Katrina, except for the celebrity factor. She and her controlling mother only royally piss me off. Whatever I once felt for her is not coming back. Maybe my accident and amnesia have made me a changed man—changed what attracts me to a woman.

"Gooch, come here," Zoey calls out, breaking into my thoughts. The high-energy canine scampers up to her.

"Now, sit," she orders with a firm hand gesture.

I can't believe my eyes. At her command, the dog instantly sits and patiently lets her attach his leash to his pink rhinestone-studded collar.

"Good boy! Ready for a walk?"

The dog wags his fuzzy little tail and whimpers, knowing what's in store.

Holding the leash, Zoey heads toward the front door.

"Wait. I'm coming with you. With your concussion, you can't walk alone."

And besides a long walk in the fresh air will do us both good given the mind-bending events that have gone down in the last twenty-four hours. I tell her we shouldn't think or talk about Frank Donatelli. She agrees.

It's been a long time since I've taken a walk in my neighborhood. I live at the top of a long, private winding road. There are no other houses along it. Just dirt, brush, and assorted wildflowers. While I've driven up and down this road numerous times since returning home, walking down it makes me really appreciate the beauty. And the beauty of my companion. Her lustrous chestnut hair shimmers beneath the early afternoon sun and her ponytail dances with the Spring-like breeze. Gucci sniffs everything and is enjoying every minute of his walk.

Halfway down the hill, I stop. A rush of déjà vu surges in my head. My eyelids flutter.

"Zo, stop for a minute."

She does as asked. "What's the matter?"

I tug at my lower lip in deep thought. "I remember something... I was here. This is where I had my accident."

She turns to me, her eyes lit up. "Yes! Do you remember it?"

Squeezing my eyes, I search my memory. My mind is a dark abyss.

"No," I say glumly, snapping my lids open.

Disappointment is etched on Zoey's face. "It'll

come back to you. I just know it will. Don't give up."

Don't give up. The words knock at the walls of my brain. They were spoken here. I'm positive.

"Zoey, did you say to me: 'Don't give up?'"

The expression on her face turns to shock. Her jaw slackens and she stammers out one word. "Y-yes." She pauses. "Do you remember anything else?"

She looks at me anxiously while I rack my brain. *Think, man, think!* I finally shake my head no. Then, I remember one more thing. I've never thanked her for saving my life.

"Thanks, Zo, for being there for me. I would have been road kill if you hadn't found me."

I wonder what it was like for her to find me unconscious in a pool of blood. The little girl who witnessed her mother's senseless murder and watched her bleed to death before drowning. Her watering eyes are a clue. A few tears escape. I brush them away, and while I savor their warmth on my fingertips, they're ripping me apart.

"Zo, stop crying"

She blinks several times. "I can't forget that day. Oh, Brandon, if you'd died, I would have—"

Almost the very words she uttered in my Bond dream! Maybe my subconscious was telling me she was the one who came to my rescue. I cut her short and put my forefinger to her quivering lips.

"Shh. I'm okay. You saved my life. I would have done the same for you."

Her glistening eyes grow wide and she gazes up at me. "Really?"

"Yeah, really." At this moment, I realize how much my assistant means to me. I need her like the air I breathe. So much I would kill for her. For a minute, the thought of Donatelli invades my brain and rage fills my bloodstream. The fucking bastard! I inhale deeply and mentally shove the image of him to the back of my head. Taking in the tranquil beauty around me, I flick Zoey's upturned nose. All sadness evaporates. She flashes her dimpled smile with those sensuous lips I've come to adore. God, she's cute. A ray of sunshine.

Gucci tugs at the leash and I chuckle. "Looks like someone's getting impatient. C'mon, let's hike some more."

We randomly turn up another desolate winding road. The uphill path is very rustic and rocky. And narrow. It cannot be traveled by car, only by foot. Paparazzi-safe. Zoey and I walk together in silence, she and the dog a little ahead of me as the dirt road isn't wide enough to accommodate the two of us side by side.

"You okay?" I ask her, amazed by the grace and ease with which she navigates the challenging path. And the way she moves her delicious ass.

"Yeah. This is really beautiful. I've never been up this way."

"Me neither." At least I think I haven't set foot here

before.

And then Zoey lets out a gasp. She's stumbled on a loose rock. I catch her before she tumbles and hold her firmly in my arms.

She exhales. "Ooh, that was close. Thanks for the save."

Letting go of her, I step in front of her. "You don't need another trip to the hospital. I'm going to lead and I want you to hold my hand." Her gaze meets mine. Before she can utter a word, I grasp one of her beautiful hands and then continue our upward trek. Gucci keeps up with us.

Stopping once to let Gucci take a leak, we reach the top of the canyon in twenty minutes. The panoramic view is mind-blowing. In one direction, we can see the Griffith Park Observatory, the Hollywood Sign, and the snow-topped San Bernardino mountains. In another, we can see downtown LA with its skyscrapers kissing the cerulean sky, and yet in another, the Pacific.

"Wow! I've never seen the ocean that color," exclaims Zoey, still holding my hand.

"Yeah. It's pretty amazing." The color really is remarkable—an intense, dense turquoise. The expanse resembles a rich panel of velvet.

Soaking in the spectacular view, we share a long stretch of silence, our hands still locked together. It's as if we've been connected like this forever. Panting, worn-out Gucci lies down.

A feeling that I cannot describe sweeps over me. It's more than just the view or the acute awareness of my companion's long slender fingers entangled with mine. So close to heaven, it's an aliveness like I've never felt before. I wonder if Zoey's experiencing it too.

Letting go of her soft hand, I gently turn her by her shoulders so she's facing me. My heart is singing and my cock is humming. With one hand, I tilt up her chin. Her milk chocolate eyes melt into mine.

"Zoey, what are you feeling?"

"The same thing you are," she whispers.

My lips descend. And then, she jerks away before her soulful eyes meet mine once again.

"Brandon, we should head back. You've got to be on the set by two and I have a shitload of work to catch up on." Her voice is thin and unconvincing.

"Right." The little dog barks—I'm not sure whether to second the motion or protest it.

We head back in silence, our hands and hearts and pasts entwined. Katrina nowhere on my mind.

My day on the set goes great. I'm rocking it. I've got my lines down and everyone's in tip-top form. The relationship between Kurt and his assistant Mel is developing, and for the first time, Mel opens up to Kurt about her own tragic past. Just like Kurt, she's lost a loved one, her own first true love, though from illness. While Kellie Fox, the adorable, talented actress playing the part, is making it so easy for me to deliver my lines, method-actor me draws from all the emotions I feel for Zoey. I put everything I feel toward her into them.

Later, after the sun sets, we shoot an action sequence on location. At a big deserted warehouse located in downtown LA. The cat and mouse game between Kurt and his late wife's assassin continues. For the first time since my accident, I hold a gun and aim it at my target. *Bang!* Let me tell you, there's nothing like having a big gun between your legs and another between your fingers you can shoot off. I channel all the rage I feel toward Frank Donatelli into my acting. The way my legendary teacher, Bella Stadler, taught me to do. The memory of this special person in my life has returned and given me a lot to think about.

The night shoot culminates with a life-or-death car chase through the dark desolate city streets with Kurt pursuing his nemesis, The Locust, in his yellow Ferrari at close to one hundred miles per hour. Adrenaline races through my veins. *Bang! Bang! Bang!* Close to midnight, we film the episode's final cliffhanger scene—a huge truck is coming at Kurt head on!

"Cut! That's a wrap," shouts out Director Niall Davies through a megaphone. "Great job, everyone. Enjoy your weekend and see you all bright and early on

Monday."

Wow. The week's gone by so fast. A PA helps me out of the car.

"You were awesome, Brandon. I can't wait to see the dailies and to find out how this season will conclude." He hands me a bottled water.

"Thanks. You're going to be surprised." The twist with Mel and Kurt professing their undying love has been kept very guarded. No one except me, the producer, the head writer, and the Conquest Broadcasting execs know about it. Even Niall and my co-stars haven't been told what's going to happen.

Doug DeMille, the show's Executive Producer, strolls over to me, and gives me a man-pat on my back.

"Great work, Brand-O."

I take a glug of the water and say thanks.

"Hey, I meant to tell you I got a call from your manager. He says you're doing *Letterman* next Thursday."

Damn. I forgot to call Scott to cancel the appearance. For the first time all day, Katrina enters my mind. I haven't missed her one iota. My mother used to tell my father when he went on his annual weekend fishing trips that absence makes the heart grow fonder. It always did for the two of them. They couldn't be wait to be back in each other's arms, big smelly fish and all. I feel nothing for Katrina except relief that she's three thousand miles away.

"That's a problem, right?" Fingers crossed he says yes because the last thing I want to do is fly to New York and freeze my ass off. Or play the Bratrina game with my fiancée and the wisecracking king of late night television. What's more, I want to stay close to Zoey and her father's investigation.

"Not at all. I spoke to the network brass, and they want you to do it. It's great publicity for you and the show. We've changed the production schedule around so you're free and clear."

Fuck.

When I get home, it's way after midnight. To my surprise, Zoey, clad in flannel pajamas, is curled up on my couch with Gucci sound asleep on her lap. The TV is on.

"What are you doing up so late?" I ask, striding toward her. I'm actually happy to see her. And even the little canine monster. They look adorable together.

"I was watching *Letterman*. Your publicist asked me to come up with some interview questions for him to ask you and Katrina."

I plop down on the couch next to her. Close enough that her cross-legged body brushes against mine. She caresses the sleeping dog's head.

"I came up with some and emailed them to her.

She's going to edit them and likely add a few of her own. She'll send you the final questions. You'll know in advance what Dave's going to ask you so you won't be caught off guard."

"Great, thanks."

"Your publicist said a couple of them are going to be about the Golden Globes."

Of course, he's going to ask how I could forget to acknowledge Katrina in my acceptance speech. The press release with my apology hasn't quenched the public's curiosity or doomsday speculations.

"You've done *Letterman* before and have always had a great time."

Not this time. "Zo, I don't want to go, but the network wants me to."

She sighs with resignation that mirrors my own. "It'll likely be your last chance to be on his show. He's retiring in the Spring. He announced it last year."

Yet another thing I don't remember. So far only scattered memories have come back. But at least I had a breakthrough at the scene of my accident.

To my relief, my assistant changes the subject. "How did your shoot go?"

I grin. It's so refreshing to have someone ask me about my day. Katrina never does. It's all about hers. The truth is I don't think I've ever had anyone in my adult life who's given a shit.

"It was awesome. I did a really intense scene with

Kellie, and she was amazing.

Zoey's big brown eyes light up. "The one where she shares the loss of her boyfriend to cancer with Kurt?"

"Yeah, that one."

"I can't wait to see the dailies."

"Ditto. And tonight, we shot an action scene downtown. A car chase. I had to fire a gun."

"Really?"

"Yeah! Major cliffhanger ending. The writers reworked it."

"Tell me!"

"When Kurt fires his gun at The Locust and says, "Get it! Got it? Good!" a big motherfucker truck heads straight into him." Not wanting to upset her, I deliberately don't mention that my rage toward Donatelli fueled my performance.

"Oh my God!"

She says the words so loudly she wakes up Gucci. His eyes pop open, and upon seeing us, he wags his tail.

Zoey immediately shifts her attention to the little dog. "Hi, cutie pie."

The little dog looks up at her with love in his big brown eyes. I gaze at her with my own puppy-eyes. Our eyes connect.

"Zo, it's late. Let's call it a night."

"Yeah, that's a good idea." She puts Gucci on my lap. "He's all yours."

Is she kidding? My cock's going to be dog food! I

freeze. To my great surprise, the dog doesn't growl or nip at me. He simply curls up. But I still don't trust him. I think he may be bi-polar. And bi-sexual.

"Zoey..."

"What?"

"If I have to sleep with Gucci tonight, I want you to sleep with me. I'm afraid he still hates my guts and will bite my nuts."

She giggles. "Brandon—"

I cut her off. "I mean purely platonically. You wear your PJs, and I'll wear some sweats and a T-shirt." I pause. "And a pair of sneakers in case the beast goes for my toes." I should probably also wear a ball cup for extra protection, I add silently.

She pets the little monster, strumming her exquisite fingers on his head. Gucci's in seventh heaven.

"Well, Zoey?"

She squirms. "I don't know."

I flick the tip of her nose. "Well, I do. I'm your boss, and if you want to keep your job, I'd be marching to my bedroom."

We're in bed. My bed.

The three of us. Me, Zoey, and The Gooch.

Each of us in some form of pajamas. Each of us on our backs. I have to admit, it's a pretty comical sight.

Especially Gucci between us, clad in his pink Hello Kitty PJs, with all four paws in the air.

There's only one problem. I can't sleep on my back.

"Zoey, roll over."

"Why?"

"Just do it."

"Fine." She hurls the word at me, and as she rolls over, so do I. Before getting squished in the middle, Gucci scuttles and curls up on Zoey's pillow. I draw Zoey in close to me until I'm spooning her. Every luscious curve of her body hugs me in all the right places. She feels warm and smells delicious. A heady blend of lavender and honey. One of my arms wraps around her supple breasts while her firm ample ass grazes the crown of my cock. I can't help it. My cock blissfully swells and brushes against her backside.

"Mmmm," I moan.

"Are you okay?"

"Yeah." More than okay. I don't think I've ever snuggled with a girl in bed. This is not something Katrina and I do. We haven't even spent a night together since my release from the hospital and I've had no desire. Katrina's body is taut, all sharp bones and angles, while Zoey's is soft, curvy, and inviting. You'd think I'd like to bury my hard cock inside her, but right now, cuddling trumps fucking. Cocooning her with my body, I feel a oneness with her. Something I've never felt with Katrina. Or perhaps any human being. Zoey's made me feel a lot of things I've never felt before with anyone. And it's the little everyday things. Be it watching TV, sharing a sandwich, or taking a walk. I'm the happiest I've been since my accident. Maybe the happiest I've *ever* been. She's made me realize the feelings that are in your heart are there forever. Even when the memory forgets. I kiss her scalp lightly.

Zoey's soft raspy voice sounds in the darkness. "Sweet dreams, Brandon."

"Same to you." I shut my eyes and hope I'm in them. Sleep overtakes me before dark thoughts of Donatelli vanquish the delicious sensation I feel.

Chapter 7

Zoey

The following Thursday rolls around quickly. Both Brandon and I are up at the crack of dawn. He's got an eight o'clock flight to catch from Van Nuys Airport. The Conquest Broadcasting corporate jet is flying him to New York. It'll land at four p.m. at Teterboro Airport in New Jersey where he'll be met by a helicopter that will take him into Manhattan. Once the helicopter lands, a limo will take him directly to the Ed Sullivan Theater where David Letterman tapes his show. Brandon and Katrina are his first guests.

"I'm all ready," he says meeting me in his bedroom where I've been packing his clothes.

I drink him in. He looks devastating. Sexy as sin. All fresh and showered, he's wearing perfectly ripped jeans and his vintage leather bomber jacket along with a cashmere scarf that matches the color of his eyes. The faded jeans and jacket are sexy enough, but there's something about the way his luxurious scarf is looped around his neck that makes him even more swoon-worthy. He looks like he's just stepped out of *GQ*. My heart pounds madly.

With a heavy sigh, I zip up his bag. Gucci, dressed in a spanking new blue sweater with a new red collar and leash, is on the bed curled up beside it. The truth is I don't want either of them to leave, especially Brandon. Aside from the Donatelli incident, the last week and a half has been the best one of my life.

While I was well enough to move back into my guesthouse by the end of last week, Brandon demanded I stay with him. That night I spent with him in his bed, though fully clothed, was amazing. He held me in his strong arms and blanketed me with his manliness, his warm breath dusting the nape of my neck and his hardness pressed against me. I fell asleep to the rhythmic rise and fall of his chest and the lull of his soft snoring. Gucci slept like a baby and so did I. Brandon made me feel safe and protected. Terrifying dreams of Frank Donatelli didn't stand a chance.

Gucci's wet kisses all over our faces woke us up early the next morning. And we giggled. Then, a phone call from Katrina checking up on her "baby boy" brought me back to reality. While he seemed aloof with her, I told Brandon I couldn't sleep with him again and that Gucci biting off his balls was no excuse. The real excuse: I didn't think I'd be able to keep my pajama bottoms on.

I cannot deny my intense physical attraction to my boss Brandon Taylor, *People Magazine's* "Sexiest Man Alive." Just one look at him sends my body into a tailspin. And the fact that I've gotten to know him this week has complicated things. It's brought me closer to him in ways I never imagined. I genuinely like him. He's smart, funny, and caring. And we seem to have so much in common even beyond Donatelli. My heart constantly thuds at the sight of him while my sex pulses with hot desire. Plain and simple, Pops is right. I'm head over heels in love with him. I'm just not sure if the feeling is mutual. He could have easily had me the other night, but except for holding me, he was totally hands off. Sleeping with him again, even platonically, will only taunt me.

Brandon protested my refusal to sleep in his bed, but I quickly played the boyfriend card. My one and only defense mechanism. It worked again like a charm, silencing him with a grim expression that bordered on a frown. And then I reminded him he's engaged to Katrina. The mere mention of her name on my tongue was like a taste of atomic sour candy. It made my mouth pucker and I wanted to barf.

This morning, he's wearing the same dour expression on his face as he nears me. With each step, my heartbeat speeds up and my knees grow weak. A shiver vibrates through me, down my spine to my toes. And there's a palpable ache between my thighs. Part of me wishes that he'd stop with whatever Mr. Nice game he's been playing with me. That he'd treat me again like his slave girl at his beck and call. The sadistic slave driver. It was easier that way.

"I've packed everything you need including your wool cap, Timberlake boots, and leather gloves." I pause, reflecting on how abnormally long it took me to pack a weekend's worth of clothes. "I've also packed Katrina's birthday present." Brandon had a PA from the show pick up my car from The Farmer's Market. Unfortunately, everything was intact. It pained me to pack the diamond necklace; I almost didn't.

"Thanks," he replies without an ounce of enthusiasm.

"I also packed the stuff you asked me to pick up at the Pleasure Chest."

Brandon flushes. "Oh, I forgot about that."

"I didn't." I still don't know why he needs a cock ring. Maybe he and Katrina are into kinky sex. The thought of that possibility kindles a flame beneath my feet like gas in a burner. I'm simmering with a mix of jealousy and lust. Even the remote possibility that there's a sexual problem between the Hollywood "It Couple" doesn't tame my agitated state.

"Oh, and I've also packed Gucci's bag. It's next to the bed."

A faint smile plays on Brandon's kissable lips. "I like the new outfit you bought him."

"Thanks. I picked it up at Petco while running some errands. I thought he should look more manly."

While the happy little dog wags his tail as if in agreement, a buzzer sounds. Brandon's intercom. My breath hitches. Gucci barks and runs in circles. The precious pup doesn't cheer me up.

"That must be your limo." I retrieve a folder from Brandon's dresser. "Here's your itinerary and the final set of questions Letterman will be asking you. Your publicist says he may surprise you with something spontaneous."

"Thanks." Brandon takes it from me and shoves it into the front pocket of his suitcase.

"I'll go open the gate. Come on, Gooch." Tucking him in one arm, I take hold of his roll away bag with my free hand and slog to the front door. Brandon trails behind me, wheeling his bag. Balancing Gucci's bag, I press a button on the wall panel by the door to open the front gate. In no time, the limo's uniformed chauffeur is at the door.

"Good morning, Mr. Taylor. I'll take your bags," says the driver, hauling both of them away.

After planting a little kiss on his head, I hand Gucci over to Brandon. God, there's something so damn sexy about the little fur ball in his arms. Tingles swarm me as he sets the dog down on the floor and then holds him by his leash.

"Take good care of him," I say, trying to mask my arousal and my gloom.

"I will. Are you going to be okay?"

My heart stutters. "Yeah. I'm going to move back into the guesthouse."

"Be careful." He holds me in his gaze, his violet eyes penetrating mine.

"Don't worry, I'll be fine."

"I'm worried about Donatelli."

"Don't be. He doesn't know what I look like or where I live." I also remind him there's a patrol car stationed outside the house 24/7.

He flashes a fleeting, semi-relieved smile. "Take the weekend off."

"Thanks." I glimpse the driver holding open the passenger door. "You better go." The words are so hard for me to say.

"Yeah, right."

We share an awkward stretch of silence. Though it's short, it feels like an eternity. The early morning air chills me.

"Watch me tonight on *Letterman*."

I force a half-smile. "I will."

I long for him to hold me in his arms. To feel his touch. The ache in my chest is so great I may break.

"Go."

With a flick of my nose, he says goodbye.

Shivering, I shut the front door and hear the limo take off.

I move back into the guesthouse and spend the day taking care of mostly personal things. Bills, laundry, emails. My pampered life is over. My gloomy mood never lifts, and as the day goes on, I fall into a deep depression. I've always enjoyed the privacy of my small living quarters, but today, without Brandon, the space feels empty and lifeless. I miss him. I fucking miss him. And that little dog too. Every menial task I attempt takes me twice as long as it should. That's because my mind is on him. I keep checking the time, hoping he'll call me when he lands. But he doesn't. Of course not. He's back with Katrina. They must be taping *Letterman.* And then, I'm sure they'll go out for dinner at some romantic Manhattan restaurant and fuck their brains out in their luxurious suite at The Four Seasons.

Perhaps due to my state of mind and concussion, I fatigue quickly. After a lame, lazy dinner of ramen noodles, I take a nap. When I awaken, I jolt. Shit. It's eleven forty-five. I hope I haven't missed Brandon on *Letterman.* I hastily reach for my remote and turn the TV on to Channel 2.

"And now give a warm welcome to our first guests,

Golden Globe winner Brandon Taylor and America's It Girl, Katrina Moore. Better known as the Hollywood power couple ... Bratrina."

Phew! Just in time. Raucous applause, cheers, and whistles erupt from the audience as Brandon and Katrina breeze onto the talk show set hand in hand. Katrina is clutching Gucci, back in one of his frou-frou pink outfits. She looks positively stunning, clad in a tight sparkling black mini dress that makes her mile-high legs look even longer in her fierce six-inch high ankle boots. Brandon, wearing the outfit he wore this morning minus the scarf, flashes his dazzling smile and waves to the audience. My heart is melting.

They take seats next to Letterman, Katrina taking the one closest to his desk. She crosses her long legs seductively and places Gucci on her lap.

Letterman: "Well, well, well. Who do we have here? Is this the ten thousand dollar dog we've all read about?"

Katrina beams. "Yes. This is Gucci. Say hello to Dave, baby boy."

The dog growls.

Letterman amusingly makes a frightened face and jolts. "Hmm, maybe you should have named him Rambo."

Katrina breaks into laughter along with the audience. Brandon twitches a nervous smile.

Katrina: "Dave, would you like to hold him?"

Letterman: "Heh-heh. Thanks but no thanks. Maybe later you'll show us one of his stupid pet tricks."

Katrina flings back her mane of platinum hair with a shake of her head. "I'd love to. He's so smart."

Letterman: "So, Brandon, how did it feel to win the Golden Globe? Were you expecting to?"

Brandon laughs. "Hardly. But it felt great."

Letterman: "Everyone's still wondering why you forgot to thank your fiancée."

Brandon squirms. Katrina butts in. "Oh! It was such a silly mistake. He's made it up to me a million times."

Letterman: "Tell us how."

Katrina: "For one thing, he bought me this beautiful necklace for my birthday."

A camera zooms in on the Elsa Peretti diamond heart necklace that's draped around her long, slender neck. She wears it perfectly. The audience oohs. A bolt of jealousy tears through me.

Brandon: "Yeah, I picked it out myself at Tiffany's."

Rage replaces my jealousy. You bullshitter!

Brandon continues. "The same place I bought her ring."

Katrina flashes a dazzling smile and her dazzling ring. Another close up.

Letterman: "Whoa! That's some rock! Six carats?"

Katrina: "Oh, Dave. You're off by four. It's ten. And it's flawless."

Letterman chuckles. "I was never good in math. So, Katrina, how does it feel to be marrying *People Magazine's* 'Sexiest Man Alive'?"

He holds up the magazine and a camera zooms in on it.

Katrina flings her mane again. "Oh, Dave. I'm so excited! It's going to be the wedding of the century!"

Letterman: "I heard it's being televised live on TV. A special edition of your reality series."

Katrina: "Yes! On Saturday, May twenty-third. We'd love for you to come." She turns to Brandon. "Right, darling?"

Brandon: "Sure. Everyone and their mother is going to be there."

I detect sarcasm in his voice. He shifts a little in his seat.

Letterman: "So Brandon, let me ask you—how do you feel about the media referring to you and your fiancée as Bratrina?"

Katrina chimes in before Brandon can say a word. "We think it's so clever. Move over Brangelina."

I want to smack her.

Letterman: "Katrina, could I share an excerpt of one of the love letters Brandon sent you before his accident?"

What! He wrote her love letters?? A painful lump forms in my throat.

Katrina: "Of course, Dave. I've kept them all."

Brandon's eyes widen while the talk show host holds up a sheet of paper that's on his desk. Letterman clears his throat.

Letterman: "Katrina, you are the moon and the stars. My whole universe. I will love you for all eternity."

The audience gushes a collective oooh while Brandon blushes. Nausea washes over me. I swallow it back as Letterman holds up the letter. It's typed, but for sure that's Brandon's signature. How many more did he write her? A sickening feeling uncoils in my stomach.

Letterman: (chuckling) "I have to hand it to you, Brandon; you're quite the poet. Do you remember writing this?"

Brandon: "Um, uh, actually no."

Katrina: "Oh, Brandy-Poo. You wrote so many you've forgotten."

The audience laughs with Katrina. Letterman joins them while Brandon breaks into a sheepish grin. The laughter dies down.

Letterman: "So Brandon, how does it feel to be working again? You gave everyone a scare with that accident."

Brandon: "I'm fully recovered. And it feels great."

Letterman: "Hey, do you mind if we show a clip from an upcoming episode of *Kurt Kussler*? My wife and I love your show. So does my son."

Brandon: "Sure. Go ahead."

The show cuts away to the clip. My breath hitches. It's the shower scene between Kurt and Alisha. Why did he pick this scene of all scenes?

My eyes stay glued on the TV screen. I relive every moment of the rehearsal shower I took with Brandon. Bile rises in my throat as a red-hot ball of fire ignites between my thighs. I have the urge to touch myself and I do. I'm a hot wet mess.

The clip fades to black and the audience applauds madly.

Letterman: "Whoa! That was intense. Do we have any more surprises to look forward to?"

Brandon grins fiendishly. "Yes. The season finale is going to end with a mind-blowing twist."

Letterman: "Since I read you're writing it, can you give us a hint?"

Brandon: "My lips are sealed."

Even I don't know what it is. He's been very secretive about it.

Letterman: "One last thing before time runs out. What are you two lovebirds doing for Valentine's Day?"

I don't recall seeing that question on the list his publicist prepared. My stomach knots up with anticipation. I totally forgot it was Valentine's weekend.

Katrina lights up. "Oh, Dave, I'm so glad you asked. Brandon is taking me to Paris for the three-day weekend! And Gucci too. Right, baby boy?"

What! He never mentioned that to me. He's taking her to Paris? The City of Love? My fingers fly off my clit while my heart tumbles as if it's been shoved off the Arc de Triomphe. A sharp pain hits me in the pit of my stomach.

I've had enough. I hit the remote. I make one call and thank God there's another man who loves me. I turn out the lights. And will myself to sleep before a volcano of tears erupts.

Chapter 8

Brandon

I've been texting, calling, and emailing Zoey every five minutes since the *Letterman* taping ended. She's back to pissing me off and MIA. Maybe Scott's right. I should just fire her sorry ass.

"Darling, can you please put the damn phone away," snips Katrina, nursing a glass of Cristal while I down a vodka martini. We're seated facing each other at a candlelit table at Cipriani, the popular downtown eatery. Gucci is on Katrina's lap, his paws on the table. While the bustling restaurant is studded with supermodels and some stars including De Niro and Pacino, all eyes are on us. Bratrina.

"I can't," I growl back at her. "I have an emergency." She knows nothing about the latest developments in my life. Pete insisted that neither Zoey nor I talk to anyone about his investigation into my hit and run and her mother's murder.

"Forget your emergency. Let's talk about Paris."

My blood runs cold. "How the hell could you spring that on me on *Letterman?*"

She smiles defiantly. "I wanted to surprise you."

"You did."

She takes another sip of her champagne. "You could show some appreciation. It's going to be divine. I've booked us the Presidential suite at the Crillon. Mommy says it's so much better than the overrated Ritz."

On my credit card, I assume. "And how are we getting there?"

"Darling, why of course, by our own private jet. We can't fly commercial with peons. We're royalty."

I assume she flew to New York on a private plane too, but truthfully, I really don't want to know. I must be at least a hundred grand in the hole, and that's just for starters because I have no idea how much she's spent shopping here.

A young, suave waiter comes by and hands us menus.

"Katrina, take a look and order me another martini. Shaken, not stirred. I'll be right back."

She shoots me a dirty look as I dart off with my phone to the men's room.

As soon as I enter, I try to get in touch with Zoey every which way I can. Goddamnit. *Nada*. I hear a toilet flush, and a dark thought besieges me.

Shit. Maybe something happened to her. With her concussion, she could have gotten dizzy and fainted... and hit her head. Or maybe she went for a swim all by herself and had some kind of spell... and drowned. And the worst thing imaginable... Donatelli showed up! My inner panic button goes off. Frantically, I search my wallet for her father's business card. Fuck. I can't find it. I've got to get home. I dash out of the men's room.

"Brandon, what's the matter?" asks Katrina as I breathlessly round our table.

"Katrina, I'm sick. I think I caught that stomach bug that's been going around."

"Puh-lease. You were fine two minutes ago."

"Well, now I'm not. I've got major diarrhea."

"Ugh!" She scrunches her face in disgust at my last word.

"I don't think I should go to Paris. Or be on a private plane with you. I've read it's highly contagious." I grip my stomach and feign pain.

"Jesus, Brandon. Absolutely. I mean, if I came down with it, I'd miss out on three days of major shopping. I have personal shoppers lined up at every store on Rue Saint Honoré from Chanel to Hermès. They're expecting me."

I intensify my pained expression and let out a moan. I'm such a good actor. But truthfully, she doesn't seem to give a damn about me. And you know what, the feeling is mutual. If I had real balls like Kurt Kussler, the character I play, I should have broken up with her on *Letterman* in front of a gazillion viewers. Unfortunately, I couldn't do that to my publicist or the network. Or my fans.

"Listen, Katrina, don't cancel the trip on account of me. You should go. Use my credit card and have fun."

Pursing her billowy lips, which look bigger than ever, she shoots me a surprised look. "Darling, what possessed you to think I would cancel our trip? Gucci and I will have a perfectly good time without you, right baby boy?"

Puzzled, the little dog cocks his head. Feeling sorry for him, I mumble, "Great. If you don't mind, I'm going back to the hotel."

With a little whimper, the dog looks up at me with his big brown puppy eyes that shout out: "Take me with you."

Sorry, Gooch. I wish I could. He belongs with Zoey and me. Scanning the celebrity-filled room, Katrina has moved on and couldn't give a shit about me. Her face lights up.

"Oh look, there's Cindy Crawford! I'm going to go over and say hello."

"I'm out of here."

It's as if she's gone deaf. Without saying another word, she leaps up and saunters off with Gucci tucked under her arm. I split. One hour later, I'm on a chartered plane headed back to Los Angeles.

Chapter 9

Zoey

Going to Palm Springs with Jeffrey and Chaz was the best thing I could have done. In addition to getting a lot of rest and relaxation, we had a blast. We sipped margaritas around the hotel pool and people watched. My hilarious companions played *How Big is His Dick?* with all the beautiful gay boys who sashayed around it. And I swam, making swimming my new passion.

Despite me telling them to go out alone for a romantic Valentine's dinner, they insisted I come along. We dined at The Tropicale, a vintage sixties restaurant that Frank Sinatra frequented, and drank pink Cosmopolitans until we were sloshed. And then we went dancing downtown at their favorite gay bar. The wild weekend away was just what I needed to get my mind off fucking Brandon.

On Sunday night, we return to LA. The drive takes about two hours. After dropping Chaz off at their downtown loft, Jeffrey takes me home.

"Want me to walk you to your guest cottage?" he asks after I step out of the car.

"Thanks, but I'm good," I say, collecting my overnight bag from him. I am, however, a little surprised that the lights in Brandon's house are on. I'm sure they were all turned off when I left. Maybe his housekeeper stopped by. And then a dark thought assaults me and sends a shiver down my spine. Maybe Donatelli's awaiting him. Or me. I give myself a mental kick and calm down. There's no way he could have gotten past the patrol car parked at the gate.

Setting my bag on the driveway, I give my brother a big bear hug. "Thanks for a great weekend. And thank Chaz again for me."

Jeffrey smacks a kiss on my cheek. "We had a great time too. Don't forget to keep us posted on Pops's investigation. I'm glad he set up police protection."

While I was in Palm Springs, I filled Jeffrey and Chaz in on everything—the latest dramatic twists with Mama's killer as well as Brandon's unexpected trip to Paris with Katrina.

"When's your boss coming back?" asks Jeffrey.

"Tuesday. Unless Katrina prolongs the trip."

"I hope they both eat bad mussels," sneers Chaz.

He makes me laugh. Though I don't wish harm on

my asshole boss, he and the bitch deserve to be buried together.

After one last embrace, Jeffrey hops into his car. As his silver Mercedes heads toward the gate, I traipse toward the private entrance to my living quarters. A stern voice stops me.

"Where the hell have you been?"

I recognize the voice instantly and spin around. Brandon! He stomps up to me. My heart races. The ache in my chest, which dissipated while I was gone, returns full force.

"I thought you were in Paris."

"I couldn't go. I came down with a sinus infection."

"You don't look or sound congested." Dressed in sweats and a T-shirt, he looks beautiful—even when livid.

"I'm better now." He repeats his question. His tone's grown angrier.

I answer as calmly as I can. "Away. If you recall, you gave me the weekend off."

"Where?" With brows furrowed, he hurls the word at me.

"Palm Springs. I went with my boyfriend. You just missed him."

"Why didn't you tell me?"

"I owe you nothing about my private life. The same way you don't tell me about yours."

He's speechless. I've called him on his Paris sexcapade with the bitch. Satisfaction sates me. Ha! It fell through. After a few moments, he breaks the silence.

"Why didn't you answer my calls or messages?" Rage still fuels his voice. "I was worried sick about you."

I think fast. "My boyfriend insisted we take no electronic devices with us. No computers, no phones. He just wanted it to be about us. Alone and romantic."

His lips pinch together. And his voice dips a pitch lower. "Where did you stay?"

"The Viceroy. The perfect place for a Valentine's getaway."

"I never heard of it," replies the amnesiac.

"It has the most amazing pool. Jeffrey and I went swimming together." I place special emphasis on the last word.

His eyes narrow. He looks as if he wishes he'd never taught me.

"We had a blast. You *and* Katrina should check it out some time."

"Thank you for the recommendation. We will."

Internally falling apart, I hold my own. "Great. And now, if you'll excuse me, Brandon, I'd like to call it a night."

As I pick up my overnight bag, he grips my elbow.

"Fine. But just one last question. Why did you bother to come back here? You could have easily stayed at your boyfriend's place."

He holds me fierce in his gaze. My eyes don't blink as I steel myself.

With a strong, steady voice I reply, "It's simple, Brandon. Absence makes the heart grow fonder."

With that, I break away from him and march to my quarters without looking back.

Chapter 10

Brandon

A *bsence makes the heart grow fonder.*
Fine. I'm going to play her little game and test out the validity of this theory.

Over the next few days, I make myself invisible. Skipping our early morning meetings over coffee, I drive myself back and forth to the set every day, and when I get home, I retreat to my office to my desktop computer. With Katrina deciding to extend her stay in Paris for a week on my dollar, my nights are not bogged down with her social events or wedding talk. Inspiration hits me. I start writing the season finale of *Kurt Kussler*—the one in which I realize I'm in love with my assistant Mel.

This is the first time I've ever written a script. I've installed a program on my computer called "Final Draft," which makes formatting easy. I'm surprised how easily the words come to me. The dialogue is a snap. I know these characters inside and out. And I've got most of the story worked out. I wrote a beat outline first which I reviewed with our head writer, Mitch Steiner, and his talented writing staff. It's so cool the way they meet regularly in what's called "the story room" and feed off each other. They were thrilled to have me among them and loved my story. They, did, however give me a few notes that I thought were great—including a more dramatic ending. Each act and commercial break must end with a cliffhanger to keep viewers glued to the show and coming back for more.

By Friday night, I'm thirty pages into it. I'm about to finish the first act. The average *Kurt Kussler* script is sixty pages long, but mine needs to be double that length as the final episode is going to be a two-hour special. The network has high hopes for it. I just hope I can deliver. My heart races as my fingers feverishly type away.

In a big turn of events, Kurt Kussler's loyal assistant, Melanie, has decided to part ways with him. Madly in love with her boss, she can't handle working for him anymore and has another job offer—to go back to the CIA. She's at his front door with her roller bag. Kurt is devastated.

KURT

Mel, you can't leave me. We're so close to nailing The
Locust

Mel looks away, teary-eyed.

MEL

I can't work for you anymore. You'll find someone
else.

KURT

There's no one like you. Please—

Kurt grabs Mel by the elbow. She jerks away from him,
her face pained.

MEL

Goodbye, Kurt. (PAUSE) You'll always be
unforgettable.

Mel grabs her roller bag and exits. The front door
closes behind her. Kurt bangs it hard with his fist.

FADE TO BLACK
END OF ACT 1

I don't think I've ever written anything so fast. My
fingers are on fire and my heart's still beating a mile a
minute. I'm feeling every emotion Kurt's feeling. The

pain. The regret. The confusion. He already knows that absence makes the heart grow fonder. It does. I fucking miss Zoey. I haven't seen her all week. Though I can't tell her a thing about the episode (I'm sworn to secrecy), I so want to share the euphoric experience I've had writing it. Grabbing my cell phone, I text her.

Have dinner with me.

I wait impatiently for her response. Nothing. I know she's home. Her lights are on. She's still playing games with me. I text her again.

Answer me.

Finally a reply:

Can't. I have plans.

I frantically type a shouty four-letter word.

WHAT?

Just as fast, a response. Another four-letter word.

A date.

Fuck her boyfriend. If I were really Kurt Kussler, I'd kill the bastard. I want him dead almost as much as I do Donatelli.

Chapter 11

Zoey

I've showered and dressed. I take a look at myself in my full-length mirror. That and taking selfies are two things I don't do too often. This time, however, my reflection smiles at me. I've got to say I look hot. Breaking the norm, I grab my cell phone from my purse—Mama's vintage beaded clutch—and take a picture of myself. Maybe I'll send it to Brandon. He's been playing games with me. Loading me up with assignments but avoiding me. I haven't seen him for close to a week. Maybe this selfie will remind him of what I look like. Or should I say, can look like.

I'm wearing the little black dress Jeffrey gave me for my birthday last year. It's one of fashion designer Chaz's creations. I never told him that it was one size too small—maybe a couple?—and I couldn't get my fat ass into it. Now, for the first time it fits me perfectly.

The tight strapless sheath hugs me in all the right places, bringing out my curves and cleavage. The six-inch black patent stilettos on my feet make my shapely legs look a lot longer. I almost feel like a supermodel—well, maybe one of those plus-size ones. I quickly gather my hair into a messy bun, sticking in a few bobby pins to hold it in place, and add a pair of cubic zirconia studs to my ears. The earrings sparkle like three-carat diamonds. No one will know they're fakes I picked up at T.J. Maxx for under ten bucks.

I glance down at my watch, my other piece of jewelry. It's a dressy thin-band one that also belonged to Mama. A gift from Papa. It's seven forty-five. Jeffrey should be here any minute to pick me up. He's arranged for a group of us to go out to a very expensive, chic restaurant—Fig & Olive. Because of my concussion, he didn't want me to drive. I told him I would do Lip Service, the latest Uber-like car service, but he was insistent on coming over.

My cell phone rings. Sure enough, it's Jeffrey.

"I'm here."

"Great. I'll open the gate." I quickly grab my treasured black clutch and head to the front door. Goddamn fucking shoes. I can barely walk in them—or the body hugging dress. Beauty is not just pain; it's a fucking pain in the ass. Before I leave, I hit a button on a pad by the door to open the electronic gate so Jeffrey can pull in.

The trek through Brandon's backyard is no picnic either. These insane heels are so hard to walk in; I'm not used to wearing them. My ankles keep buckling. It's a shame my klutzy walk doesn't match my sexy attire. I almost trip three times. Once so close to the pool, I almost fall in. Thank God, I know how to swim now.

My walk of death to the driveway feels like an eternity. When I finally get there, Jeffrey's silver Mercedes convertible is parked outside. The top is down. My breath catches. He's standing next to it... and so is Brandon. Oh, Jeez. I wasn't expecting this.

Managing to stroll up to them as gracefully as I can, I immediately throw my arms around Jeffrey and give him a kiss. Wearing a stylish slim suit and his hair slicked back, he looks movie star handsome. He and Eddy Redmayne could have been separated at birth.

"Hi, babykins," I say, breaking away. It's time to put those acting skills back into play. I mentally pray: *Please, Jeffrey, play along.* Just to be sure, I clasp his hand and dig a heel into his foot.

"Ow."

I quickly turn to a puzzled Brandon and plaster a big smile on my face. "Brandon, you remember my *boyfriend*, Jeffrey." I put special emphasis on the word "boyfriend."

Brandon's face is pinched. Narrowing his eyes, he gives Jeffrey the once over. "Yeah, sure."

"Good to see you, again." Jeffrey extends his hand.

With reluctance, Brandon shakes it, and I silently sigh with relief. Jeffrey's gotten the hint. I turn to Brandon and melt at the sight of him. He looks hot as shit—barefoot in a relaxed V-neck T-shirt that shows off his biceps and low-slung gray sweats that subtly enunciate his breathtaking endowment.

"What are you doing out here?" I don't know why I'm making conversation with him. The sooner I get out of here the better. I'm heating up.

"I heard the gate open and then saw a car drive in on my surveillance monitor. I wasn't expecting company so I stepped outside. Why didn't you tell me your boyfriend was coming by?"

An angry tone accompanies his question.

"I told you I had a date." *Asshole.*

His eyes rake over my body. I swear he's mentally undressing me.

"You're very dressed up."

You could say I look nice!

"Are you going somewhere special?"

Jeffrey chimes in before I can respond. "Yes, Fig & Olive."

Shit. I wish Jeffrey hadn't told him where we're going. Too late now.

Brandon knits his brows. "Hmm. That's a very expensive restaurant."

He can afford it, jerk! Remember, I told you he was

rich.

Smiling his own dazzling smile, Jeffrey replies. "It's a special occasion."

A mixture of curiosity and suspicion sweeps over Brandon. "What are you celebrating?" The tone of his voice is confrontational, as if he has the right to know everything about my personal life.

Jeffrey's smile turns mischievous. "It's a surprise."

"Oh." Brandon's voice is small, almost deflated.

I turn to Jeffrey and brush his clean-shaven jaw. "Sweetie, we should get going. We don't want to lose our reservation."

"Agree." After saying goodnight to vexed Brandon, he opens the passenger door and I slide into the convertible. I catch Brandon's eyes on my very exposed thighs before Jeffrey closes the door and hops behind the wheel.

On my next breath, Jeffrey turns the car around and motors toward the gate. Via the side mirror, I can see Brandon heading back into his house. An unexpected forlornness washes over me. I should be excited about going out for a fun evening with Jeffrey. But the truth is I'd rather be home, curled up on a couch, watching *Kurt Kussler* episodes with the man of my dreams.

Fig & Olive on nearby La Cienega is a chic, super-popular restaurant, especially with the Hollywood elite. I've made numerous dinner reservations at it for Brandon. This, however, is my first time here. I'm awed by the number of expensive cars pulling up to the valet. A parade of Bentleys, Ferraris, Porches and more. Jeffrey's Mercedes fits right in.

Inside, the restaurant is pure Hollywood glamour. Sleekly modernist, it's packed with the most beautiful people I've ever seen. They exude power, money, and sex. I even see several stars among them. It makes sense this is a restaurant Brandon and Katrina frequent. The power couple known as Bratrina belongs here.

The stylish blond hostess, who could be a starlet or supermodel herself, leads us through the bustling restaurant. Following her, I feel self-conscious. I'm definitely the biggest woman here. Jeffrey, on the other hand, is totally comfortable, and along the way, several patrons warmly say hello to him. He's definitely now on the A-list, being the number one event planner in LA.

We end up at a round table in the back corner of the restaurant. Enjoying drinks and engaged in lively conversation is Jeffrey's boyfriend Chaz and a small group of their close friends. I immediately recognize Blake Burns from the Internet and Chaz's twin sister, Libby, whom I've met a few times before. She's curvy like me except she seems so much more comfortable in her skin.

"Hi, everyone," beams Jeffrey. He then introduces to me to Blake and his charming wife Jennifer, who he affectionately calls tiger. Jeffrey and I take the two vacant seats. Chaz is to Jeffrey's right; I'm to his left. I notice they're each wearing identical diamond earrings. They look a lot like my cubic zirconias, but I bet they're real. Both Chaz and Jeffrey make a boatload of money. Their businesses have been very successful.

A dashing waiter brings by a bottle of expensive Dom Pérignon. Popping the cork, he fills everyone's flutes until there's no more champagne to pour.

The waiter disappears and Jeffrey raises his glass. "We've brought all you lovelies together to share some very exciting news…Chaz and I are getting married."

Raucous whoo-hoos erupt before we toast them. My heart fills with joy. I'm so happy for both of them, especially my brother. I never thought he'd find the right one. But according to both of them, it was love at first sight when they met at Jeffrey's former employer—Enid Moore, of all people. Katrina's mother.

I take a sip of my bubbly and before it goes down, my stomach lurches. I practically choke it all up. All eyes are on him as he marches my way, taking one long angry step after another. He's still dressed in his sexy sweats and barefoot. He could wear a garbage bag and he'd still be ungodly gorgeous. Every muscle in my body quivers, and my heart hammers like a jackrabbit's. Still coughing, I set the glass down before it tumbles out of my hand. Our eyes make contact and I can feel him shooting poison darts at me. Bull's-eye. One after another, they hit me hard in my chest.

"Zoester, are you okay?" asks a concerned Jeffrey.

"I don't know," I mumble after a fit of coughing. An explosive mixture of shock, rage, and apprehension courses through me like a Molotov cocktail. The asshole fucking followed me here!

"Well, hello, Zoey," he says frostily as he steps up to our table.

Before I say a word (as if I can even get one past the giant lump in my throat), Blake Burns jumps up and gives Brandon a man hug. "Hey, man, great to see you here."

After another guzzle of her almost all-consumed champagne, chirpy Libby chimes in. "Hi, Brandon. Why don't you join us? We're having a celebration."

"What are you celebrating?" His voice is as cold as dry ice. His menacing eyes don't stray from me.

"My brother Chaz's engagement."

Chaz gives a little wave.

Oh, no! I'm about to be busted. *Quick, Zoey!* Change the subject.

"Don't you think the weather is—"

Loose-lips Libby cuts me off and rattles on. "He and his boyfriend Jeffrey are getting married!"

"That Jeffrey?" Brandon's bugged-out eyes flick to my brother and then shift back to me. They hold me

fierce.

Oh shit! Kill me now. I want to crawl under the table.

Tipsy Libby grins. "Yes."

Oh dear God, what must he be thinking??!! I leap to my feet. I need to escape. "Brandon, why don't I find a waiter to bring over a chair?"

"No need. I won't be staying and neither will you." In a quick heartbeat, he grabs me forcibly by the elbow and wrenches me away.

"Wait! I have to go to the ladies' room!" *And stay there for the rest of my life.*

"Excuse us," he says calmly to my dinner mates, ignoring my excuse. "I have a crisis and need to borrow my assistant."

"What the fuck are you doing?" I yell, no longer in earshot of my friends.

"Your fucking boyfriend?" he barks back at me. Squeezing my upper arm, he herds me through the restaurant at breakneck speed. Every eye is on us. Every step is a stumble.

"Slow down! You're going to break my ankle!"

"Then I'll carry you out of here."

He squeezes my arm tighter and picks up his pace. If he weren't holding on to me so hard, I'd be on my ass.

"You're hurting me!" I protest at the top of my lungs.

"Oh, you're such an expert on hurting people," he growls.

We're outside before I can respond. His fancy Lamborghini is parked, with the top up, is parked in front of the restaurant. He probably tipped the valet extra to leave it there.

With two clicks of a remote control that he's holding in his other hand, the Lambo doors fly open like beetle wings.

"Get. In. The. Car." He shoves me inside it and then hops into the driver's seat. He slams a button on the dashboard. The vertical doors fold down and automatically lock. I'm trapped.

"Jesus, Brandon!" I fumble for my seatbelt. Before I can fasten it, he grips my hands so tightly I yelp.

"Let go of me!"

"Turn around and face me, Zoey."

"No!"

"Do it, Zoey, or I'll do it for you."

Slowly, I turn to face him. His violet eyes are still blazing with fury.

"Who the hell is that guy?"

"M-my brother."

"Pete's kid?"

I nod. While I mentioned Pops and Auntie Jo had a son when I told him about my family, I deliberately never revealed his name.

"Why did you lie to me?" He fires the words at me.

"I-I don't know." My voice wavers.

"To make me jealous?"

My silence is his answer. Shaking, I'm so close to bursting out in tears I can taste them.

His gaze burns a hole in me like acid. And then his face softens just a little. "You know what, Zoey? You're smart. You're funny. You're cute. You *should* have a boyfriend."

Me? Smart? Funny? Cute? My body clutters with flutters.

"Um, uh," I stutter until he shuts me up without warning.

His luscious mouth crashes onto mine like a meteor. My body is sparking; my heart's on fire. Swirling colors explode behind my eyes. The kiss is open-mouth, savage, and all-consuming. He cradles my face in his palms, heating my cheeks and deepening the raw, hot kiss with his deft tongue. Anchored in place, I melt into it, losing myself to him with each potent stroke. Moans fill my ears as I tear at his T-shirt, and he gnaws at my lips. Arrows of arousal shoot to my sex. I can barely breathe. There's no other word for it. Possession. He's taken complete and utter possession of not only my mouth but also of every cell in my submissive body. And then as fast and unexpectedly as he initiated the fierce kiss, he breaks it, leaving me bereft and confounded.

"Why did you do that?" I pant out, my heart pounding, my pussy pulsing with need.

"To show you what you're missing out on."

"Oh." As I squeak out the little word, my eyes lower and then grow as round as marbles. Holy shit! He's got a beast of a boner. It may even burst through the fabric of his sweats.

He tilts my chin up with his thumb, pressing hard against my tender skin. His eyes burn into mine, glinting with mad lust. "I'm not done with you."

My just-kissed lips quiver. My body shakes. My throbbing clit aches. Oh my God! Is he going to fuck my brains out? Right here in the car?

"Zoey, you need to be punished." His voice deepens and a Satanic look sweeps over his face. "And I'm going to be the one to do it."

He jams a key into the ignition, and on my next heated breath, we peel away from the curb with a roar.

A short ten minutes later, we're almost back at his house. A tense silence prevails as he zooms up the narrow winding streets, expertly navigating them. Entering the gate, we pass the patrol car on duty. Brandon zips into the garage and parks next to the Jag. Apprehension and anticipation are still whipping through my veins as he clicks open the Lambo's switchblade doors and undoes our seatbelts. Rounding the vehicle, he grips my upper arm and drags me into his house. It's pitch black, lit only by the glitter of the city below. The dark silence is mesmerizing, almost haunting.

Letting go of me, he sinks into his sofa. His gorgeous face is shrouded in shadows. His violet eyes glow. I stand there motionless like a statue, too scared to move a muscle or say a word.

"Zoey, have you ever been spanked?" His voice is pitched low, almost melodic.

"No," I mumble. Mama and Papa didn't believe in that kind of corporal punishment. Nor did Pops or Auntie Jo.

"For taunting me, you need to suffer the consequences. A good spanking is what you need."

My heart is in my throat. I gulp it down. A curious blend of tingly erotic sensations swarms me. Fear gives way to desire. I *want* him to spank me. Badly.

"Are you okay with that?" he queries.

I silently nod like an automaton. I *more* than want him to spank me. And I want him to give it to me hard. My throbbing clit is begging for it.

A wicked smile curls his lips. "Good. Then, please come here and get over my knees."

As if induced into a trance, I do as asked. His hard muscular thighs press against my abdomen and I can feel his gigantic rock-hard erection against my pulsing sex. My arms are folded on a cushion, my head buried between them.

"Perfect," he growls as he shoves my tight dress up above my ass, leaving my thong, a mere piece of butt floss, intact. I can feel his eyes on my bottom.

"You have a gorgeous ass, Zoey. It's a shame you don't have a *real* boyfriend to appreciate it."

I'm too entranced to say a word.

"This is going to hurt. I want you to choose a safe word and use it if it becomes too much for you."

Shit. I can't get my mind to work. Or my mouth to move. *Think, Zoey, Think.*

"Well, Zoey…"

"Please," I murmur. Mama's magic word.

"Any word but that."

"Mama," I say without overthinking it.

"Excellent. Now, tell me, Zoey, you'll never lie to me again."

Before I can I get my mouth to move, a firm hand crashes down on my right cheek. I feel the sting as the sharp sound echoes in my ears. A moan escapes my mouth.

He hits me again, this time harder. "Zoey…"

"I'll never lie to you again."

Slap! "Zoey, show a little respect. Say: 'Sir, I'll never lie to you again.'"

My voice a tremor, I do what he asks.

"Now, apologize for lying to me."

Slap! I wince. "I'm sorry."

"Not good enough." Another swat of his hand. "You're missing a word."

"I'm sorry, *sir.*"

"Apology accepted. But you need something more as a reminder to NEVER lie to me again."

Without warning, his large hand crashes down on me again. I scream out. And then again. And again and again. Tears sting my eyes and I whimper. He picks ups his pace and spanks me yet harder, faster. Always in the same spot. Over and over. My ass is on fire. My whimpers morph into sobs. Loud, soulful wails like the cries of an animal in heat. Scorching tears sear my face and forearms. My sobbing intensifies, washing out the harsh crackle of his hand upon contact with my raw burning flesh, deafening me, arousing me, setting every ounce of me ablaze.

"Zoey, no more playing games. No more testing me. Do you understand?"

I nod like a bobblehead doll, unable to get a single word out.

"Zoey, I need words."

"I understand, sir." I manage, my voice a mere croak.

And then suddenly, I feel his powerful knees press hard against me. They bounce me into a standing position, but as I rise, my knees buckle beneath my legs. Clasping my waist, he catches me before I collapse onto the floor. Heaving, I let him hold my limp body in his arms.

"Shh, baby." Still holding me firmly in one arm, he lifts his other hand and smooths my hair. "Why didn't you use your safe word?"

"I'm sorry," I sob out from my quivering lips. Hot tears continue to stream from my eyes.

"No, I'm sorry." His voice is soft and compassionate. "Did I hurt you?"

"A little," I lie. Yes, it hurt like hell, but I loved every erotically charged minute. My safe word was nowhere near the tip of my tongue.

"Come here." Wordlessly, he draws me in closer until my breasts graze his chest. My sensitized nipples pucker beneath my dress, sending another rush of wetness to my sex. His rock-hard cock presses against me as he caresses my sore butt. His tender touch is so soothing. The pain mixes with pleasure. Still in stilettos, I rest my head against his pecs. My eyes clamp shut as his heartbeat drums in my ear like a sweet lullaby. My crying subsides.

I don't know how long we stay in this position until his sultry voice awakens me from my state of nirvana. I gaze up at him. His eyes are hooded and a faint smile plays on his lips. With one hand, he brushes away my remaining tears. Thank God, I wore waterproof mascara. One hot wet mess is enough.

"C'mon, let's get you back to your party. And let's forget this ever happened."

I nod, knowing I will *never* forget this moment. This experience. Commiting it to memory, I catch my breath.

Five minutes later, we're back in his sports car. This time he drives down the twisting, hilly roads slowly, meandering as if he never wants our journey to end. And truthfully, neither do I. "All of Me" plays on the radio. The lyrics fill my head and my heart.

The painful truth hits me like a rockslide. I turn my head toward him, glimpsing his intensely beautiful profile. A runaway tear trickles down my face. Yes, all of me loves all of him.

"Go," he says stoically as he drops me off.

The elegant dining room of Fig & Olive is still filled and bustling. Adjusting my dress, I stumble back to my table. Jeffrey and his friends are in the middle of eating dinner. Everything looks and smells delicious, but I'm not hungry.

"Zoester, where'd you go?" asks Jeffrey as I take my seat.

I fumble for an excuse. "Um, uh, I had to help Brandon with some lines. He had a panic attack." I blink several times, holding back confused tears. My intuitive brother's gaze stays on me, and from the look on his face, I can tell he's concerned. He knows how I feel about Brandon.

Chaz, who has no clue, looks at me shrewdly. "C'mon, Zoeykins. You really want us to believe that? You have that just-fucked look going on!"

"Honey, leave her alone," says Jeffrey to no avail.

Mortification races through me. My face is flushing. I hastily take a gulp of my still there bubbly. Chaz's comment elicits a heated reaction from the clearly buzzed group.

I defend myself. "No way would I sleep with my boss."

"That didn't stop, my tiger," chimes in Blake before giving his wife an affectionate peck on the cheek.

"Blake!" shrieks a reddening Jennifer. "Say no more. And that goes for the rest of you too."

Chaz snorts with laugher. "Okay, I won't tell anyone about how you two fucked in Blake's fuck pad at the Conquest Broadcasting Christmas party."

It's Blake's turn to look embarrassed while the others roar with laughter.

"C'mon, Zoey, tell us the truth," begs a loaded Libby, the penultimate market researcher who's always asking questions and seeking answers.

I take another sip of champagne. "It *is* the truth." *Kind of?* Unless zipless fucks count. "And besides, Brandon's engaged to Katrina Moore." The taste of her name on my tongue nauseates me.

"Bratrina!" sneers Chaz.

In unison, the others mimic him. My brother, however, clasps my free hand under table, giving it a knowing, affectionate squeeze. As much as I love and can confide in him, I'll never tell him what transpired tonight between Brandon and me.

Libby cuts into her steak. "Poor Brandon."

Poor me. I'm drowning in self-pity.

Chapter 12

Brandon

"**D**rop to your hands and knees!"

"But, sir!"

"Private Hart, you are not to question my orders. Now do it!"

Clad in a camouflage pattern lace bra that pushes up her voluptuous breasts and a matching G-string, she obediently gets down on all fours, shoving her sweet ass up in the air. Her face is flush from just giving herself an epic orgasm. Her gorgeous, curvaceous body trembles at the perilous possibilities ahead.

Admiring her sensuous beauty, I loom over her. I'm in a drill sergeant's uniform, wearing polished, knee-high leather boots and wielding a whip in my hand. Sergeant Taylor, my newest role. I crack the whip against the floor narrowly missing her. The sharp thwack is like music to my ears.

"At-ten-tion!" She arches her back and looks up at me, her lips quivering with fear and anticipation. The hungry look on her face for the pain I'm about to inflict brings my dick to attention. The power between my legs infiltrates my entire body.

"Private Hart, you disobeyed me. What happens to naughty little soldiers who don't listen to their commanders?"

"They get punished...sir."

I crack a wicked smile, pleased she's addressed me properly. "That's right. You must pay the price of coming before I said you could. Did you forget I'm in charge and your orgasms are under my command?"

"I'm sorry, sir."

I smack my lips and shake my head. "When will you ever learn? Do I have to send you back to Boot Camp for more basic training?"

"Please, no!"

"No, who?"

"S-sir."

Gulping, she bows her head in submission and doesn't see it coming. With an iron fist, I swipe the leather whip against her ripe ass. She winces and arches. I stand back and admire my handiwork. A pink streak welts up on her exposed tender flesh.

"Now give me fifty."

She looks up at me again with those imploring big brown eyes in search of forgiveness. Mercy's not part of my vocabulary. I give her another sharp lash. *Whoosh!* Then another and another. She whimpers, then weeps. Tears fall at my feet, a few clustering like dew drops on my shiny boots. The rhythmic thwacks of the whip clash with her hitched, harsh sobs, creating an erotic symphonic cacophony. I can feel the heat rise from her burning cheeks. A canvas of intersecting bas-relief lines in fifty shades of pink has turned her ass into a priceless masterpiece. My cock is raging. It may burst through my khakis. I have to have her, but I exert control.

"Now, move it!"

Wordlessly, she begins to do push-ups. Those pathetic, wimpy, girly kind. But I love the way her big tits graze the ground and the way her scrumptious ass moves up and down with each successive pump. I badly want to fuck it...good and hard.

"Let me hear you count, soldier. Start from one."

"One...two...three..." By twenty, she's breathless and trembling with fatigue. Sweat clustered on her chest, she gazes up at me with urgency.

"Private Hart requests permission to stop."

"What's the magic word?"

"Please, sir, please!"

Fuck. I love when she begs. "At ease. Get up on your knees."

With a breath of relief, she kneels before me. Her flushed chest rises and falls, her plump tits stirring with lust. Oh, what a beautiful sight! I dangle my whip and dust the tip across each nipple, one after the other. She moans. As they harden into two mini torpedoes that want to shoot through the lace fabric of her bra, my cock strains.

On my next breath, I yank down my fly. My big gun springs free. A weapon of mass destruction, it's level with her impassioned face. I splay my big hand on the top of her head and urge her to take it. I hiss as her warm mouth wraps around the crown.

"Take it all," I bark.

Obediently, my good little soldier goes down on it, trailing her tongue along the thick rigid shaft. Oh, yeah. I've trained her well. I clench my fists by my sides and groan each time it hits the back of her throat. I could easily detonate at the base and coat it with a full load, but I've got other plans. My cock's wet and ready. I withdraw and circle behind her before getting down on my knees. My big, glistening erection brushes against the two adorable dimples centered above her red-checkered cheeks. Pursing my lips, I bend over and blow a cool breath on her raw, rosy flesh.

"Does that feel good, Private?" I breathe against her fiery backside.

"Oh yes, sir!" she gasps.

"What about this?" One hand slides between her splayed thighs and makes its way to her pussy. Fuck. She's so hot and wet. I've aroused her as much as she's aroused me. Pressing my thumb on her throbbing clit, I plunge two fingers into her slick slit, shoving them deep inside until my fingertips touch the warm flesh of her womb. She lets out a soft moan.

I slap her sore ass. "Answer me, soldier. How does it feel?"

I jab a little harder. She gasps.

"I need words."

"Oh, so, so good, sir!"

A smirk curls on my lips. "That's better."

I run circles around her clit with my thumb, turning it into a hard nub. More moans and groans escape her throat.

"Oh, please, Sergeant Taylor, fuck me."

I yank back her head by her ponytail and meet her heated gaze. She yelps.

"Careful. I give the orders." I tug again at her mane. "Is that what you want? For me to fuck you hard?"

"Yes, sir." Her voice is a desperate rasp.

It's time to get down to business. I'm so fucking turned on. Releasing her silky hair and withdrawing my soaked hand from her slickness, I rub my hard as nails dick with her pussy juices, lubing it further. Using both hands, I spread her rosy cheeks wide and aim it at her opening. My hand wraps around my enormous pulsing shaft, and inch by thick inch, I barrel into her tight puckered hole. She winces. I hiss. So fucking good. Oh, yeah, she's going to get it hard. So hard she'll be begging me to stop. But I'm going to fuck her brains out. Fuck her to oblivion before she can cry out her safe word. Clutching her hips, I begin to pummel her...

CUT! Fade to black.

My alarm goes off. The end of another kinky wet dream. *To be continued*. My eyes snap open and I shakily sit up. The covers are torn off me. I have a raging boner. And I know why. I can't get my assistant, Zoey Hart, out of my head. She's literally and figuratively under my skin. I dreamt about her. Relived last night's spanking in a crazy, cinematic fantasy. Jesus. Sergeant Fucking Taylor. Wielding a whip. Fucking her ass. How far will I take my sexual proclivities? My need for dominance? My need to possess her?

Last night should have never happened. But it did. It was all about control, but I'm the one who lost it. Jealousy fueled my rage and rage fueled my dominance which fueled my need to punish her. Sure, I told her to forget about the spanking, but that's not going to be easy. It's going to be next to impossible. The same for me. I wish I could blank it out. Bury it in the vortex of my amnesia. I dread facing her and can't fathom how we'll continue to work together. Now what? Maybe we need to talk about it.

Rolling out of bed stark naked, I stagger to the bathroom. Usually by the time I get to the toilet, my morning wood has started to go down. Not today. I stare at my monstrous boner and swear it's laughing at me: "Ha, ha, ha, I'm not going anywhere." No way can I pee in the toilet with it. My huge erection shoots out of me like a torpedo, perpendicular to the floor. Desperate for relief, I hop into the shower, turn on the water, and take a whizz, shooting my stream straight at a glass wall. Then, I jerk off, fantasizing her beautiful fingers curled around my dick. For sure, they're long enough to circle all the way around it. With a loud grunt, I come.

Towel-drying myself, I think more about last night. Part of it felt so wrong, yet everything felt so right. Why can't I stop thinking about her? Hopefully, a swim will help me chill out. Clear my mind. And make it easier to face her.

Zoey is setting my Starbucks on a table when I finish my last lap. All the tension I eliminated with my swim dives right back into me at the sight of her. Dressed in a tight T-shirt and jeans, she looks fresh and sexy. My cock stirs. She's still affecting me, and I can't make the feelings and sensations she arouses go away. It's hopeless. Damn her. Hoisting myself out of the pool, I grab my towel and throw it over my shoulders. Heading her way, I have no clue what to say. And my arousal isn't helping. It's only making things worse.

"Here's your coffee." Her voice is devoid of emotion, and she's deliberately avoiding eye contact with me.

"About last night—"

She meets my gaze. "There's nothing to talk about. What I did and what you did was wrong, but two wrongs don't make a right. You were right, however, about one thing. I need a boyfriend."

I feel totally deflated. It's as if she has no feelings toward me. Her tone is very business like, bordering on icy.

"Zoey, I have feel—"

She cuts me off again. "Please, Brandon, let's not talk about it. Like you said, let's forget about it and move on. Your schedule is on the table. You're shooting the entire day. It may go into overtime."

I notice there's no coffee for her. Usually, she sits with me and reviews my schedule, but obviously, she's not going to do that today. Guess what? She *is* affected. She's just not letting on. She's a damn good actress. I feel a glimmer of hope.

"Yo, Brand-man. How's it going?"

A familiar nasal voice interrupts my thoughts. An unexpected visit from my manager, Scott. Wearing a navy blazer over cream pants and an open shirt, he ambles our way. His leathery skin looks tanner than ever. For sure, he's gone to one of those tanning salons.

Zoey's expression hardens at the sight of him. Her father's been working day and night to uncover the connection between him and Donatelli, the motherfucker who murdered her mother and also did in my parents. But so far, no leads. Scott still denies ever having lunch with him. Plus he has an alibi: After having lunch with Katrina at The Ivy, he accompanied her to a bridal gown fitting at nearby Monique Hervé's eponymous boutique. The designer backed him up as did Enid, Katrina's wedding planner mother, who was also there.

Zoey and Scott exchange scathing looks. Their mutual disdain is palpable.

Zoey: "Excuse me. I have a lot of things to take care of."

"Nice seeing you too, sweetheart," Scott snickers as my assistant pivots on her heel. My eyes stay on her as she traipses back to the guesthouse. My X-ray vision penetrates her jeans. I can see that gorgeous ass. And that delicious cheek is still red. My cock flexes. It's as if it's telling me there's no such thing as mind over matter. Damn it. She's fucking with my brain.

Scott takes a seat. "Mind if I have a smoke?"

I do mind, but I let him. He reaches into the breast pocket of his blazer and pulls out a pack of Camels and his gold lighter. Scott really seems to like gold. He's wearing a thick gold chain that hangs low on his hairy chest and a pinky ring with a substantial diamond. He lights up a cigarette and inhales. I'm relieved he blows the smoke away from me.

"Scott, why are you here?" Though he's been my long-time manager, my relationship with him since I awoke from my coma has been on shaky ground. I don't like the fact he's shown up here uninvited.

He takes another drag of his cigarette. "I have something to ask you."

"I want to ask you something first."

His face tenses. "I thought we were done with that Farmer's Market incident. And I'm going to level with you. I don't like the smell of that cop on my trail. What's his fucking problem?"

You. But I keep my mouth shut. Pete's instructed both Zoey and me to not talk about it with him or make any mention of the fact that we know he lied when he told me he called in my accident. I tell him I don't know why he's being investigated and assure him my query has nothing to do with the incident. I brave my question.

"Did I ever share anything about my sex life with Katrina before my accident?"

"You told me it was off the charts hot. And Katrina told me the same thing. You two were going at it like bunnies."

I don't know whether to believe him. Since discovering he lied to me about my accident, I can't trust him. All is not what it seems.

"Have I always been honest with you?"

"You've never held back." He takes another puff and then flicks the ashes on the patio. Fucking slob. I should get him an ashtray, but by the time I get back, there'll be a mountain of ashes. No point.

"Was there anything else she or I told you? Anything unusual?"

He puffs again on his cigarette. "Other than she likes to be on top?"

I'm getting nowhere with him. It's strange he knows what she likes but has no clue about my kinkiness. I'm definitely not going to tell him about it. Or that I've been having wild sex dreams about my assistant. Even when I'm not dreaming about her, I fantasize about spreading her legs and bending her over. Making her come a thousand different ways and hearing her scream out my name. Oh, that pretty mouth. So beautiful when it opens wide. Wide enough for me. In my mind's eye, I picture it wrapped around my massive shaft, sucking, licking, and sending me over the edge. I feel my cock swell beneath the table.

"How did it go in New York?" asks Scott, bringing my focus back to him. "It's too bad you couldn't go with Katrina to Paris."

I squirm in my chair, painfully aware of the ache between my legs. I'm going to tell him the truth and gauge his reaction.

"Katrina and I still aren't getting it on. And I still

don't have any feelings toward her."

Scott's jaw tightens. "Well, you sure could have fooled me on *Letterman*. The two of you rocked it. It was one of his highest rated shows ever. The public can't get enough of Bratrina. Fan mail has been pouring in everywhere—CBS, Conquest, and at Celebrity-TV. The world can't wait for you and Katrina to tie the knot."

My stomach twists. The words spew out.

"I'm having second thoughts."

Scott's cigarette practically falls out of his mouth. "What the hell are you talking about?"

"Maybe we should postpone the wedding until my memory comes back."

Scott's left eye twitches while his face darkens. "You're out of your fucking mind. You're talking career suicide. Listen, Brandon, just get the hell married and everything will come back to you."

Maybe he's right. He nervously takes another puff of the cigarette and then blows out an offensive cloud of smoke in my face. He goddamn better not give me cancer.

"Scott, do me a favor. Put out the cigarette."

A troubled expression washes over his face. He tosses the cigarette butt to the ground and stamps it out.

"Listen, Brandon, let's change the subject. I came over here because I have a personal favor to ask of you."

"What?"

"I need to borrow a couple grand. I'll pay you back."

I digest his words. I just paid him his weekly salary. Twenty grand. He needs more money?

His anxious eyes stay fixed on me. His left eye is twitching considerably. More than before.

"Sure," I say, no questions asked. "I'll write you a check when we go inside."

He smiles with relief. "Thanks, Brand-man. I appreciate it."

Five minutes later, we're in my office. I unlock my safe and pull out my large checking ledger. Transporting it to my desk, I sit down and make out a check to him in the amount he requested. Two thousand dollars. With my felt-tipped pen, I write "loan" in the memo before signing it. Somehow, I think I'm never going to see the money again.

While I tear it out of the ledger, my manager eyes my computer screen. "How's the script going?"

Shit. I didn't close the file on my desktop. I've got to be more careful. The story is top-secret. Not even my manager can know about it. Especially one I don't trust. I hastily stop what I'm doing and shut down the computer.

"Good," I stammer as the screen goes blank.

While I finish with the check, Scott sets his leather briefcase on the corner of the desk and unzips it.

Overstuffed, it tips over and the contents splatter onto the floor.

"Fuck," Scott mumbles, under his breath. He squats down to gather the assorted papers. Jumping up from my chair, I join him. The repulsive scent of his cloying cologne and smoke-filled clothes wafts up my nose.

"Thanks, man," he says, stuffing his briefcase.

Helping him, I eye what looks to be an itinerary that includes a round-trip three hundred dollar ticket to Vegas and a three-day stay at The Venetian. He's departing tonight. Not making mention of it, I slip it into his briefcase. He throws in the last remaining papers and a fallen box of Camels and then zips up the case. We stand up in unison.

"Don't forget this," I say, handing him the check.

"Yeah, thanks again, man." With jittery fingers, he shoves it into the breast pocket of his jacket. "I'm gonna be out of town for a couple of days, but call me if you need anything."

"Good luck in Vegas," is what I want to say, but I bite my tongue. There's a reason why he didn't volunteer his destination.

As soon as he's gone, I call Pete and tell him about Scott's mysterious trip to Sin City. "He's on Southwest Flight 389 departing tonight at 7:50 from LAX."

"Me and the missus haven't been to Vegas in a while." I can picture Pete smiling on the other end. "Thanks for the tip."

My next call: Zoey. I share the news with her. To my surprise, her voice is flat and emotionless. Almost cold.

"Thank you for letting me know. I'm sure Pops will keep me informed."

She hangs up.

That's not the only time Zoey hangs up on me. Since the spanking incident, the dynamic in our relationship has changed. She avoids me as much as I avoid her, and when we do see each other, we avoid eye contact. I wish I never spanked her. I crossed the line. It was totally unprofessional. Yet, I think she enjoyed getting it as much as I enjoyed giving it to her. She refuses to talk about it.

It's been three days. Zoey's become totally closed off. I can't even share her father's latest findings about Scott. He's a big gambler. Likes to play blackjack, the slots, and craps. Donatelli, however, was not spotted anywhere in Vegas. Pete's not any closer to nailing Zoey's mother's murderer or solving my hit and run.

Whenever I begin a conversation, she merely says, "I know" or gives me the cold shoulder and walks away. Her emails and texts are equally terse. Every rejection of one of my advances shreds me. On Tuesday, Zoey delivers my Starbucks in the morning while I'm in the pool doing laps. I've decided I'm going to have a come to Jesus meeting with her. Enough with this shit. I want my assistant back. The way she was before. But when I emerge from the water, she's gone. The sound of a car peeling out of my driveway screeches in my ear. What the fuck? Sopping wet, I hurry to the table where I've left my cell phone and where she's deposited the Starbucks bag. I speed dial her. No answer. I text her. No answer. I call again. No answer. She's playing games with me again, and it's pissing me off. Mad as hell, I reach into the bag for my caffeine fix. To make me madder, there's no coffee. Only a note scrolled in her elegant handwriting on a paper napkin.

Brandon~

I'm taking some time off. I'm using my vacation time. Please do not call or text me. I won't answer.

~Zoey

PS I don't know when I'm coming back.

I crumple the napkin in my fist. I'm so blood-curdling mad I can feel steam coming out of my nostrils. I should just fire her sorry ass. But I can't. I love that ass. And that's not all I love about her. I love her curves, her big brown eyes, those kissable lips. Her fire and pride. The way she laughs and makes me laugh.

Fuck. She's under my skin and in my bloodstream. She's everything Katrina isn't. I relive the spanking. How she submitted to me yet stayed so strong. Obeyed without questioning. She's awoken my sexual desire and made me realize I need to be in control. Dominate. With Katrina, I can never be in control. She submits to nothing and to no one. Including me. She's either pussy whipping me or busting my balls—and that's when she's not as frigid as Lake Michigan in the winter. How could have I fallen in love with her? Was I different before my accident? Did my accident change me?

A familiar voice cuts my thoughts short. "Brandon, that bitch assistant of yours almost ran into me!"

Damn. Katrina. She's back from Paris.

I wish Zoey had.

I don't know when I'm coming back.

A horrible thought hits me. Panic grabs me by the balls.

Zoey's leaving me.

Chapter 13

Zoey

I'm heading back to that spa outside Joshua Tree. The one that slimeball Scott banished me to, of all places, while Brandon was comatose in the hospital. Call me nuts but don't shred me. As much as I loathed it the first time around, it's exactly what I need right now. An escape. It was relaxing; it made me think clearly, and I shed a few pounds.

On the lonely drive down the 10 Freeway, I call only one person, knowing once there, cell phones are banned. Get caught with one and say goodbye to both the phone and the spa. Pops picks up on the first ring.

I tell him I'm taking a vacation.

"Are you having a problem with Brandon?" he asks, always so intuitive. My father knows how I feel about my boss and is convinced it's mutual. I don't agree.

"No, Pops. I just need to get away for a few days."

Far away from him.

"Where are you off to?"

"To the Vipassana Wellness Center. Don't worry, Pops. It's a retreat in the middle of the desert. I'll be safe. Have you found out anything more about Scott?"

He updates me. Pursuant to his trip to Vegas with Auntie Jo, he conducted an investigation into Scott's finances.

"Is he in debt?" My detective mind is at work.

"It's hard to tell. All his credit card accounts have been closed, and he only uses debit cards. While his bank account is relatively small, he's got substantial assets—including a two million dollar condo, a place in Aspen, and a fancy yacht. Plus, I learned Brandon pays him a heftier salary than you thought."

"Like what?"

"A million bucks a year."

"Wow!" I seriously didn't think it was that much. Rage whips through me. The douche deserves shit. Fucking asswipe!

"Interestingly, he asked Brandon to borrow some dough."

"How much?"

"Two grand."

My heart sinks. Like Pops, I know that's not enough to raise an eyebrow. With his hefty salary, Scott can easily pay him back.

"Do you think he owes Donatelli money?"

"Don't know. But killing Brandon off wouldn't solve the problem. He'd be literally cutting off the hand that feeds him."

Frustration peppers Pops's voice. "I can't connect him to Brandon's hit and run. He says he never left his Wilshire Corridor condo until late afternoon—way after the accident. The doorman corroborated this as did the building's surveillance camera."

"What about Donatelli?" I ask, feeling less and less hopeful.

"Zippo. We can't trace him. He covers his steps all too well."

When it comes to detectives, Pops is the best of the best. Yet, he can't get to first base with either Mama's case or Brandon's hit and run. I know how defeated he must feel.

"What about Katrina?" I ask impulsively.

"She's in the clear and has an alibi too. She says she was at her mother's house. Her mother backed her up."

What was I thinking? With all she stands to gain from marrying Brandon, she's the last person who'd want him dead.

"Pops, did you show her the green glass heart?" It's the one unusual thing that Pops found at the scene of Brandon's accident. While I think it belongs to some local jogger, Pops is convinced it belongs to the person responsible for his hit and run.

"There's a prob—"

"Pops, you're breaking up. I can't hear you."

Shit. As I turn onto the 29—the Palms Highway—I lose my connection. Even if I could keep my phone at the spa, chances are I wouldn't get service so deep in the desert.

With a leaden heart, I soak in the scenery. Though I'm not far from the Palm Springs hotel where I stayed with Jeffrey and Chaz just a week ago, this feels like a million miles away from civilization. Driving in silence, I pass miles and miles of exotic cactus, geologic rock formations, and spiky, twisted Joshua trees that look like they belong in a horror movie. In the distance surrounding me, the snowcapped Santa Rosa and San Jacinto mountains glow umber under the setting desert sun. It's almost surreal.

Twenty minutes later, a campus of unpretentious adobe buildings rises from the desert landscape. I've reached my destination and pull into the entrance. I check in, surrender my phone, and then retreat to my quarters in the women's building.

The room is small and utilitarian. It's actually closer to being a jail cell than a room at a spa. There's just a cot, a set of drawers, and a bathroom—a perk for returning "students of life." Newbies have to use a communal one. I quickly unpack and put away the few things I've brought along, mostly yoga pants and tees plus my swimsuit, and call it a night. Except I don't fall asleep. Fucking Brandon's in my dreams. And I'm fucking him.

Over the next few days, I set out to accomplish what I've come here to do. The spa is renowned for offering peace and tranquility, quietude and beauty. Rooted in a form of meditation that originated in ancient India, Vipassana is a refuge for the human spirit, self-discovery, and healing. Each morning after a sparse breakfast of blended organic juices, I retreat to a meditation room and meditate. As I sit cross-legged on a mat surrounded by a dozen other similarly posed individuals, I focus on my breathing and try to cut him loose from my conscience. But I can't. All this visualization crap is backfiring. His gorgeous face fills my mind as I contemplate my resignation letter:

Hi Brandon …
Yo Brandon …
Dear Brandon …
Dearest Brandon …
My Dearest Brandon …
My Beloved Brandon …
Hey Dickhead …

Tears sting my eyes. I can't get past these words. Vipassana means seeing things for what they really are. After three days, it's as clear to me as the desert sky—I can't leave him. I'm addicted to him … in love.

I make it through a week. Meditating and juicing. On my eighth day in the late afternoon, after a vile green liquid lunch that I can barely swallow, I retreat to the heated mineral pool that's like a grotto in this giant mosaic of nature. Using the techniques Brandon taught me, I swim laps and laps until I lose track of time and all I can think about is lifting my head out of the bubbly natural spring for a breath of air. After about an hour, I get out. The desert sun beats fiercely and I relish the heavenly clean air. I don't even need a towel to dry myself. Invigorated from my long swim, I take a seat in one of the Adirondack chairs that surround the pool. I close my eyes and let my bones soak in the heat. Aah! It feels good.

When I open my eyes, I find an older woman sitting next to me in a wheelchair. Her thick silver hair trails down to her waist in a loose braid, and though gaunt, her strong, defined features with cheekbones like apples tell me she must have once been a great beauty. A light cotton blanket covers her. I notice that she shakes. The more I look at her, the more she seems familiar. But even with my eidetic memory, I can't place where I've seen her before.

"Hello, my dear," she says. Her voice is husky and theatrical. "I enjoyed watching you swim laps. You have lovely form."

I smile. "Thank you. I had a great teacher." The memory of Brandon teaching me how to swim floats into my head. I can feel his strong arms holding me in the water and then wrapped around me after I completed my first lap. I can almost hear his heartbeat in my ears though we're miles apart.

The woman smiles back at me. "I used to be a teacher. But, now due to my health, I only occasionally instruct classes at my school."

"What's wrong with you?" I venture, instantly regretting my words.

But the woman is not offended. "I have advanced Parkinson's. I come here once a month with my nurse for the special Ayurvedic spa treatments they offer."

"What exactly are those?"

"A variety of mineral massages and herbal hydrotherapies as well as a special organic diet specific to Parkinson's sufferers. The treatments originated in ancient India. They help halt the progression of the disease though I'm not sure if they can cure it."

"I'm sorry," I say, for lack of something better to say.

"Don't feel sorry for me, my dear. I wake up happy every day of my life. I've lived a full life and have no regrets." She holds me in her warm, soulful gaze. "So, tell me, why are you here?"

Be it that I feel so cleansed and clear-headed or that she makes me feel so comfortable and I have the need to talk to someone, I open up to her.

"I've been having a problem with my job."

"Are you an actress? You have such an interesting voice and a lovely way of projecting it."

"Hardly. I'm the personal assistant for someone."

She shoots me a knowing smile. "Ah, so you're in love with your boss."

I flinch. "How did you know that?"

"My dear, it's written all over your face. I'm a master of reading emotions. What is the conflict?"

"He's engaged to someone else. They're getting married in May."

"How do you know he's in love with her?"

"He bought her a gazillion dollar engagement ring and a magnificent necklace for her birthday."

She lets out a deep throaty laugh. "My dear, those are just material things. Does he hold her hand? Caress her face? Flick her nose? Brush away her tears? Carry her in his arms?"

All the things Brandon does to me. "No," I say with a small shake of my head. While I've had the misfortune of witnessing a blowjob, I've rarely seen Brandon being affectionate with Katrina.

"I came here to get him out of my system. A cleanse, I guess. But when I meditate, I only think of him and when I go to sleep, he's always in my dreams."

The woman nods. "Then your stay here has served its purpose. That is your clarity."

"What do you mean?"

"Let me ask you. Do you want to work for someone else?"

I shake my head again. "No. I only want to give

myself to him."

"Has he ever demonstrated that he cares about you?"

Delicious memories dances in my head. Taking that shower with him fully clothed... dressing him for the Golden Globes... being swooped up into his arms after coming home from the hospital... the spanking. As much as I want to share them with this wise woman, I simply nod and whisper "yes."

She takes my hands in her frail trembling ones. "My dear, actions speak louder than words. The smallest gesture can convey so much more than the biggest word. Even just the touch of a hand."

My mind flashes back to the first time I met Brandon... how, when our fingertips met in the pouring rain, all the thunderstorms in the world couldn't put out the fire that raged inside me. And then my mind jumps to our hike up the canyon with little Gucci. The touch of his hand when he took mine connected me to his soul and core. A slight desert breeze sends a row of goosebumps up my arms.

"What should I do?" I ask this bastion of wisdom, my voice so small. "I can't stop dreaming about him being mine."

"My dear, I have always told my students *not* to follow their dreams. *Lead* them and land them. Go back to him and fight with your heart for what you want. If it's meant to be, it will happen."

I digest her words. In the distance, a petite but sturdy brown-skinned woman with a long shimmering black braid heads toward us at a brisk pace. She's clad in a colorful sari.

"Miss Stadler," she says in a melodic, Indian-accented voice, wrapping her fingers around the handles of the wheelchair. "It is time for another treatment."

Miss Stadler? Brandon's mentor? Could it be?

"I hope I'll see you again, my dear," the beautiful, disabled woman says cheerfully as she's whisked away by her nurse.

I'm too stupefied to say anything. Is this all meant to be?

One hour later, I'm packed. I've collected my phone, and I'm on my way back to LA.

Chapter 14

Brandon

INTERIOR KURT'S KITCHEN-NIGHT

The lights are dim. KURT'S at the counter, pouring himself a glass of Scotch. Shirtless, he's wearing sweats and looks unshaven and disheveled. He takes a few sips and tosses the glass to the floor. It shatters.

KURT

Goddammit. I'm falling apart without her.

ANGLE ON THE KITCHEN DOOR
The knob twists and the door opens slowly.

CUT BACK TO KURT
He pivots and his eyes narrow in disbelief.

KURT

What are you doing back?

As I pound out the line, I say it out loud. I'm about to write Mel's comeback when my name sounds in my ear. A soft familiar rasp. On my third shot of whiskey, I'm in a drunken haze. I must be imagining things. I whirl my desk chair around and blink hard.

"Hi."

It's Zoey, with her overnight bag in hand. In my stupor, I didn't hear her drive in. Her glimmering eyes meet mine. I'm taken aback. How many agonizing days has it been? Five? Seven? Ten? It feels like an eternity. I've lost count. In fact, I thought she'd never come back. Dressed in stretchy yoga pants and a *Kurt Kussler* sweatshirt, she looks rested and thinner. I can tell even in the dimness.

"How was your vacation?"

"Enlightening."

She glows like an angel under the overhead halogen light. At the sight of her, my comatose cock awakens with a stir. It wants to steal my next line.

"I missed you."

She quirks a smile. "I swam a lot."

I smile back at her. She doesn't move. We share a stretch of silence. Only the electricity between us is palpable. I can hear the sparks.

"What are you doing?" she finally asks.

"Writing."

Her eyes warm with interest. "Oh, the *Kurt Kussler* season finale?"

Though I never told her I was doing this, she must have read about it in the trades or online. My writing debut has been highly publicized.

"Yeah. But, I can't really talk about it." Damn. I hate being sworn to secrecy.

While I'm dying to share the plot twist with her and show her what I've written, I'm grateful she doesn't pursue the subject. Her eyes fix on the almost empty bottle of liquor.

"You should stop drinking."

We share another awkward stretch of silence. I so want to take her in my arms and taste her. Wash away the foul taste of the whiskey with her sweetness. "Do you want anything to eat or drink?"

She turns on her heel. "I'll bring you your Starbucks in the morning."

"I'm going to take a break. Are you sure?" The truth is I'm famished. Dealing with bouts of depression and writer's block all week, I haven't eaten much.

At the doorway, she cranes her neck and looks over her shoulder. "Yeah, I'm sure. Just keep writing. Don't give up."

At her last three words, something in my head clicks. My eyelids flutter. And my heart races.

"Zoey!" I call out her name. It's too late. She's

gone.

I swivel my desk chair and face the computer. I feverishly type away. I know at last how the season finale is going to end.

"Cut! That's a wrap!" shouts out Director Niall Davies.

While just minutes ago, a loud gun explosion thundered in my ears, now an explosion of claps, cheers, and wolf whistles reverberates. On location, we just finished shooting the last scene of the explosive season finale of *Kurt Kussler*. The emotionally charged cliffhanger that dramatically changes the dynamics between Kurt and his assistant Mel.

Lying in a pool of make-believe blood on the street just outside Kurt's house, I slowly sit up. Wiped out, I swipe at my face, burnishing the tears my co-star Kellie Fox shed. Still crying, she's kneeling beside me.

"Are you okay?" I ask.

Her eyes continue to water. Then, laughter mingles with the tears. "Brandon, you got to me."

I brush away her tears and then smack her mouth with a kiss. My lips long to be smothering another mouth. The mouth I thought about everywhere on my body while shooting—and writing—this climatic, action-packed episode.

I compliment my co-star. "You were amazing."

She truly has been. This has been a breakout episode for her. While Kellie's always been terrific, the depth of emotion she's shown from start to finish has been astounding. She made the lines I wrote jump off the page and come alive. I wouldn't be surprised if she gets an Emmy nomination for Best Supporting Actress in a Drama Series for her moving portrayal of Kurt's assistant, Mel.

A cheek-to-cheek smile spreads across her face. "You were too. Thanks for writing such an incredible script."

I think that may be the best compliment I've ever received from a fellow cast member. In writing the script, I learned the power of words. How each one can make a significant difference. Orgasmic elation sweeps over me.

Kellie reels me in. "Are Kurt and Mel going to get a happily ever after?"

A sudden cloud of doubt falls over me, shrouding the euphoria.

"I don't know." My voice wavers. *I really don't know.*

Before I can say another word, the congratulatory crew surrounds us. I help Kellie to her feet as we both stand up. My shirt is completely soaked with fake blood.

Our ecstatic Executive Producer, Doug DeMille, offers to take everyone out for drinks at a nearby

Mexican cantina.

Shrugging off my shirt, I politely decline.

I just want to celebrate with my inspiration.

The woman whose heart eludes me.

My Zoey. Zoey Hart.

Chapter 15

Zoey

The next few weeks are the happiest I've ever seen Brandon. That's *when* I see him. He spends long hours on the set, shooting the season finale of *Kurt Kussler*. It's a closed set, so no one but the cast and crew are allowed on it. To my further dismay, I can't even help him with his lines because the storyline is top-secret. I'm dying to know how the season ends, but Brandon is tight-lipped about it. Everyone's working overtime to get the two-hour feature-length episode shot and edited in time for MIP. It's going to be shown at the convention to an exclusive group of international broadcasters. Brandon's traveling to Cannes along with network production chief, Blake Burns, the producers, and the rest of the cast to participate in a Q&A panel discussion following the screening. He's flying to France via the Conquest Broadcasting private jet and staying in a suite at the 5-star Carlton Hotel. Lucky for me, I don't need to set up his flight or accommodations; it's all been handled by the Conquest travel department. Unlucky for me, Katrina's probably tagging along. I can't imagine her missing a red carpet opportunity.

After the shoot, I see Brandon even less. He spends long hours in editing, rising early and coming home at ungodly hours. I've never seen him so involved with an episode. I miss seeing him. But I don't miss seeing him with Katrina. To her frustration, Brandon, with his crazy hours, has had no time to deal with all the wedding details. It's taking place a few weeks after he returns from Cannes. I'm besieged with nasty emails from her, insisting I get Brandon to focus. After I forward some of these emails to him, he tells me to just agree to all her demands. I reluctantly obey his orders. Each time I reply to her, I feel a pin prick my heart.

In every email, she rubs it in that the wedding is going to be a live televised spectacle—a special edition of her reality series, *America's It Girl*. I wish I could forget, but that's been next to impossible. Promotions for it are everywhere—from billboards on Sunset to backs of busses. The whole world will be watching the two of them exchange their forever vows. While I promised Brandon I'd be there, I still don't think I can stomach it. Whenever I have my doubts or a down moment, I turn to the inspirational words his mentor, Bella Stadler (yes, it was her for sure!), shared with me at the wellness spa about leading and landing your dreams. Maybe I'll go and, just before they exchange their "I do's," work up the courage to object. The thought of doing that on national TV scares the hell out of me.

Just about the only time I see Brandon is in the early morning—after his daily swim. Not only do I bring him his regular iced Grande Caffè Americano, but also an iced vanilla blended to drink at the editing sessions. The episode is being edited at a nearby Hollywood facility.

"How's it going?" I ask him about two weeks in after he sits down next to me at a patio table.

Fresh out of the pool and dripping wet, he takes a sip of his iced coffee. My eyes stay fixed on his glistening well-formed bicep that flexes as he holds the cup to his luscious mouth. Oh, those exquisite long fingers! And then, my gaze shifts to his gorgeous face as he imbibes the chilled dark brew through a straw. His violet eyes twinkle like two morning stars while he sensuously licks his upper lip. Tingles fly through me like glitter as he meets my moonstruck gaze.

"Do you have a passport?"

"Yeah, why?"

"You're coming to Cannes with me."

The words spin around in my head like a pinwheel in the wind.

"Come again," I stutter, my jaw slackening.

"You heard me. I want you to come to Cannes with me."

My heart is pounding so loudly I'm sure he can hear it. I've never left the country except for a daytrip to Tijuana with my brother Jeffrey. My souvenir—a major case of Montezuma's Revenge. Setting the coffee on the table, Brandon continues.

"We finished editing the season finale of *Kurt Kussler* last night. As you know, Conquest is screening it at MIP. I want you to attend the gala premiere with me."

I can't get my brain to communicate with my larynx. Brandon Taylor has just given me the best invitation of my life. Every ounce of my being is doing a happy dance. Then, an invasive thought brings me crashing down from my high.

"Isn't Katrina going with you?"

He playfully flicks the tip of my nose. "She can't. It's her father's sixtieth birthday. She's going up north to visit him in prison."

I almost like her for a minute. Then, on my next breath, I love her so much I'm giddy.

"When are we leaving?" I ask with unbridled excitement.

"In two days. You'll be flying with our executive producer, the cast, and me on the Conquest corporate jet. Blake Burns and his wife Jennifer will also be flying with us."

Holy cow! Visions of walking down the red carpet with him dance in my head. I'll be like a movie star. Paparazzi abounding. But there's only one problem. Gah!

"Brandon, I don't have anything appropriate to wear."

He tips up my chin with a thumb and shoots me that panty-melting smile. "Don't worry about it. Right after I shower and dress, we're going shopping."

"B-but, I have a million things to do."

"You have nothing to do. Just get ready. Barneys opens at ten. End of discussion." Taking his coffee with him, he strides to the back entrance of his house, leaving me a hot, wet, excited mess. As soon as he's no longer in sight, I leap to my feet and actually do one crazy happy dance. Whoo hoo! I'm going to Cannes with Brandon!!

Barneys in Beverly Hills is bustling with chic, affluent-looking men and women, who obviously have nothing better to do than shop for clothes, shoes, and makeup at ten o'clock in the morning. The stunning women all look like they wear size zero. Clad in chic all-black ensembles or tight-ass designer jeans, they fit in perfectly with the store's glistening black and white marble décor. All eyes are on gorgeous Brandon, who looks like he belongs here, and on me, who looks like something the cat brought in, my hair a Medusa-like mess from driving here in his vintage Jag convertible. I feel out of my element. Target or T.J. Maxx is where I belong.

Brandon eschews the winding stairs for the elevator off the perfume department. It's packed. Several pencil-thin, stylish women, who look like they could be supermodels, say hello to Brandon, and stare at him seductively. They're probably former hook-ups—just his type. A few suspicious eyeballs stay riveted on me. I can read their minds like a magazine: What is *she* doing with him? I face forward to avoid eye contact and eagerly await the elevator doors to part. Brandon allows the other passengers to exit first when we hit the second floor.

"Are we getting out here too?" I ask as they file out.

"Yup. This is the Designer Floor."

Tingly goosebumps sprinkle over me like fairy dust when he takes my hand. His grip is warm and firm.

"C'mon, Zo. I've got a personal shopper lined up who'll get you everything you need for Cannes."

Holy shit! A personal shopper. My excitement comes to a screeching halt as I step out of the elevator.

"Why darling, fancy meeting you here!"

It's Katrina, dressed to the nines in a sleeveless black mini dress that's complemented by matching stilettos and a monstrous designer bag. Her perfectly coiffed platinum hair cascades over her shoulders as if she's just come straight from a high-end salon. Behind her, are two weary sales associates. One is clutching all-in-pink Gucci, who wags his tail at the sight of us. The other is wheeling a rack of extraordinary designer dresses. Sparkles abound.

Brandon lets go of my hand before she notices. Katrina flings her toned arms around him, completely ignoring me. Smiling, she turns her head toward the overflowing rack of clothes. Dozens of glittering jewel-toned gowns hang from it, packed like shimmering sardines.

"These are all the dresses I've selected to wear on my show over the next coming weeks and on our honeymoon."

At the word honeymoon, my stomach bunches. I anxiously watch as she yanks one of the dresses off the rack. A strapless persimmon Armani. I glimpse the price tag—twelve hundred dollars.

She holds it up against her. "Darling, this is the dress I'm going to wear when I visit Daddy. I'll show the world that orange is the new black my way."

"That's great." Two monotone syllables.

Katrina bats her feline green eyes. "Brandy-Poo, since you're here, would you like me to give you a fashion show? Mommy's going to be here, too, any minute."

"Can't. I have something important to do."

Spoiled brat Katrina looks miffed. "And what might that be?"

She still hasn't said a word to me. It's like I don't exist. I wonder—does she know I'm going to Cannes with Brandon?

"I need to help Zoey pick out a wardrobe for MIP since she's coming with me."

Well, she sure as hell knows now. In the blink of an eye, the expression on Katrina's face goes from questioning to cold fury. She slaps her manicured hands onto her jutting hipbones as her jaw drops to the marble floor.

"What!? You're taking that fat peon to Cannes?"

"Yup," says Brandon matter-of-factly. "And please don't *ever* call her that again."

"Are you out of your mind? She's a total embarrassment."

I clench my hands by my sides so I don't punch her in the face. Or pull out a clump of her hair. A catfight with America's "It Girl" at Barneys would not look good. It would definitely be all over the Internet by noon.

"She's going to assist me," adds Brandon. He refrains from telling her that I'm attending the red-carpet premiere of the *Kurt Kussler* season finale.

Katrina calms down with a haughty fling of her hair. "Very well. But you're wasting your time here. There's nothing in this store that would fit her fat ass."

"Katrina! Apologize! Do it now!"

"Puh-lease."

Gucci growls at her.

I feel myself reddening with rage and want to scratch her eyeballs out. But dammit, she's right. I don't belong here. And I don't want to be ridiculed by some obnoxious salesperson. I need to get out of here as fast as I can. And then *ping!* A light bulb goes off in my head. Why didn't I think of this before?

"C'mon, Brandon. Let's go." I step back into the elevator. Brandon follows me. I pound the ground floor button.

"Brandon, where the hell are you going? We need to talk!" shrieks Katrina.

The doors close in her face, catching her orange dress. She screams, "Open up!" as the elevator descends. So long, bitch!

Five minutes later, Brandon and I are back in his car, heading downtown.

In no time, thanks to unusually minimal traffic and Brandon's need for speed, we're in downtown LA at Chaz's fabulous new showroom. After his former studio, in a rundown building, virtually evaporated in an electrical fire, Jeffrey raised the funds to relocate the studio to the hip Arts District and make his fiancé's studio a showcase—a sleek, vast modernist space that mirrors the aesthetic of his designs. It's way beyond what his insurance claim would have covered.

"Zoeykins, let's get this show rolling," gushes Chaz after a big hug and learning about my trip to Cannes. "This is so exciting."

While he scurries to put together a new wardrobe for me, Brandon plops down on an oversized white leather chair. He leans back, folds his arms across his chest, and gives me the once over. My skin prickles everywhere.

"What size are you?"

My heart skips a beat as my eyes flick to the model-sized mannequin in the corner of the studio. I scan her long sculpted legs, narrow waist, jutting hipbones. Katrina!

My eyes shift back to Brandon. Cocking a brow, he shoots me an unnerving look. "Well…"

"I'm a size…"

Six! I so want to say six.

"S-s…"

Brandon taps his foot impatiently.

"S-s…" The number is on the tip of my tongue.

"S-size…" I vomit the next word. "Ten."

To my horror, I swear he mentally undresses me and then to my surprise, smiles approvingly. "A perfect ten."

The next hour is ripped from the pages of a fairy tale. A medley of Meghan Trainor songs blasts out of concealed speakers, followed by Mark Ronson's "Uptown Funk." I parade out of the dressing room, wearing one outfit after another, each one more fabulous than the one before. I effortlessly and sexily move to the beat of the music. Strutting my stuff with hip moves that rival a supermodel's, I feel like Julia Roberts in *Pretty Woman* though she's far from my size and four inches taller. Brandon just sits there, sexily slouched, legs spread apart, and either nods approvingly or gives a thumbs up. He's enjoying every minute of my show. Much more than he lets on. It's hard to miss the visible bulge between his legs. I'm fucking turning him on! And the truth is I'm turned on like a fire hydrant. I may need to buy a new pair of panties to replace my drenched ones.

By noon, I've line up over two dozen outfits for MIP—ranging from sequined mini dresses and gowns to chic jeans and a super-sexy tux outfit similar to the one Rihanna wore on the Grammy's.

My brother's exuberant fiancé beams. "Zoeykins, you're going to rock it in Cannes."

Brandon's eyes travel from my face to my toes, lingering on parts of me he has no right to be staring at. He flashes his trademark cocky grin.

"Yeah, she is."

Chapter 16

Brandon

Taking Zoey shopping for clothes is the most fun I've had in ages. I've never done that before to the best of my recollection. I mean, taking a woman shopping. By this time, the experience would have triggered a memory. My memory's coming back to me at the speed of an avalanche, though I'm constantly thrown off course by things I can't remember. One thing's for sure, I've never taken my fiancée Katrina on a shopping spree. She's perfectly capable of doing that herself. I banish the thought of her before she spoils all the fun.

Zoey's so fucking sexy as she models one seductive outfit after another. Halfway through her—or should I say my—fashion show, inhibition gives way to exhibition. She's practically a Gloria's Secret super-model as she struts out of the dressing room in a sparkly body-hugging violet gown with a thigh-high slit that accentuates every curve of her sensuous body. It's definitely what I want her to wear to the *Kurt Kussler* season finale premiere at MIP... and then I will rip it off of her curvy little body as soon as I can. Yup, that's the plan. My cock couldn't agree more and applauds her as she does her spin.

Zoey changes back into her jeans. While she's in the dressing room, I remember one more thing she'll need for Cannes.

"Chaz-man, do you by chance have a woman's leather jacket lying around?"

Chaz grins. "You're in luck. Hang on."

My eyes follow him as he scuttles over to one of the racks filled with heavy woolen clothes made for colder weather. In no time, he's back, holding up a hanger with a snazzy brown leather jacket draped on it.

"This is my Jazzy-Chazzy motorcycle jacket. It's a sample from my Fall line."

I smile. "It's perfect. We'll take it. How much do I owe you?"

"Forget it," he says. "The publicity I'll get with Zoey wearing my designs is priceless."

"Are you sure?"

"Totally."

"What about a charity I can contribute to?"

Chaz's eyes light up. "That would be awesome. How 'bout my friend, Gloria Zander's organization—

Girls Like Us? It's a non-profit that helps neglected and abused girls find a positive course in life."

While Zoey's never been neglected, the senseless murder of her mother to me was abusive. So, this charity makes sense.

I write out a $25,000 check while Chaz organizes the garments I've selected. The best money I ever spent. And an added surprise. Gloria Zander, the founder and CEO of Gloria's Secret, will undoubtedly send over a boxful of sexy lingerie and shoes to match all the sexy dresses as her own special thank you. The skimpier the better I tell Chaz. I also tell him to keep the delivery anonymous. He shoots me a conspiratorial wink.

Cannes awaits us. I have a week to spend away from Katrina. To figure out who and what I want in life. My heart gallops. I think I already know. Despite my amnesia, my mind's never been clearer. Should I tell her before we leave?

Chapter 17

Zoey

Pinch me. I've been living a dream from the minute the Conquest stretch limo picked Brandon and me up at his house and transported us to LAX to meet our private jet. Wait! I take that back. Don't pinch me. I don't want this dream to end.

I've only been on a plane a few times before. A crammed Southwest flight to Vegas and another to San Fran. The economy cabin stunk of sweat and beer, and I was sandwiched between my tray table and chair like a slab of raw meat. Efficient. Yes. Luxurious. No.

The Conquest corporate jet is the most luxurious vessel I've ever traveled on. Yes, I've seen private planes in countless TV shows and movies, but nothing has prepared me for the experience of flying on one. The interior is all soft beiges and rich woods, with spread out plush leather chairs that can fold back into sumptuous beds. There's even a dining cabin and a complete bar with the finest crystal and silverware. Champagne flows and we're served gourmet meals on monogrammed Conquest china.

I recognize everyone on board from having met them on the set of *Kurt Kussler*. Brandon, nonetheless, re-introduces me. Go-to-Zo, his personal assistant. While the reality of my subservient position drives a screw into my gut—that's all I am—everyone treats me with respect. They couldn't be nicer.

Soon after takeoff, Brandon leaves his seat and mingles with the guys. I, in turn, enjoy chatting with Blake Burns's wife Jennifer, who I met at Jeffrey and Chaz's engagement party, as well as with Brandon's co-stars, Jewel Starr and Kellie Fox. Kellie tells me the season finale is to die for. I can't wait to screen it with Brandon. While Jewel and Kellie move on to chat with Jewel's husband Niall about tomorrow night's festivities, I spend more time with Jen.

The more I talk with her, the more I like her. She's super sweet and asks me a lot of questions about myself including where I grew up and how I came to work for Brandon. I'm somewhat in awe of her. Besides being so pretty and married to one of Hollywood's top television executives, she's super successful in her own right. About the same age as I am, she started a women's erotica channel—MY SIN-TV—and has single-handedly made it a huge success. I try to hide my inferiority complex. Here I am, almost twenty-five, and I'm just a lowly assistant. And she's running a network.

"Do you have career aspirations?" she asks over champagne.

Taking a sip, I tell her I thought about getting into acting but had to abandon that dream because it was too risky and financially challenging for someone like me.

"You're adorable!" she counters. "You should reconsider. I'm going to keep my eyes and ears open for any parts that might work for you."

Wow! I thank her from the bottom of my heart, and the conversation switches to Jeffrey and Chaz.

"I'm so excited about their wedding," she gushes.

"Me too."

She goes on to tell me that she and Blake have offered to let them exchange their vows in the expansive yard of their new Santa Monica house.

"I'm sure it's going to be an extravaganza. A total showcase for my brother's event planning talents."

"All the better." She smiles. "He made my wedding unforgettable."

She goes on to explain how Jeffrey worked with her creative husband Blake to transform her parents' backyard into a winter wonderland in the middle of July. As she spews the details, a tinge of melancholy nips me. Growing up, Jeffrey was forever planning my dream wedding, acting it out with Barbie and Ken, but as I grew older, I knew that was a long shot. In fact, now I seriously believe it'll never happen. The man of my dreams is engaged to another. And truthfully is way out of my league. I shoot him a glance; he's in a serious conversation with Blake. I wonder what they're talking about.

As much as I'd like to ask Jen to tell me more about Katrina, I don't broach the subject. From Chaz, I know she despises Brandon's fiancée as much as I do. The bitch almost came between her and Blake. In fact, she almost cost Blake his life. I still haven't shared this info with my boss. Jen doesn't bring up Katrina either. A nice girl from Boise, she was probably raised with the value: "If you don't have anything nice to say, don't say it at all." Growing up with brutally honest Pops and Jeffrey, I was taught to tell it like it is. I internally sigh. I so wish I had the nerve to tell Brandon what I know about the crazy bitch. Just maybe I will.

Chapter 18

Brandon

"The season finale looks fucking amazing," says Blake after taking a sip of the expensive Scotch we're both drinking. "That ending is killer—no pun intended."

"Thanks," I say proudly. "And thanks for believing in me and letting me write it."

"We have high hopes for it. Libby Clearfield, our research head, has been tracking intent to view and the score keeps going up every day. Ninety-eight percent of your viewers say they won't miss it. There's even considerable interest among non-viewers. The buzz is sensational. We anticipate the ratings to go through the roof."

"Wow," I say, both humbled and blown away.

"We'll get our first feedback when we screen it tomorrow night."

I take a sip of my drink. "I'm a little nervous."

Dressed casually in jeans and a T-shirt like me, Blake laughs and gives me a warm pat on the back. "Don't be, man. It's going to rock and the Q&A afterward will be a piece of cake. I'm moderating it so there's nothing to worry about."

"Great." I imbibe more of my Scotch and swallow just in time before Blake pops a disquieting question.

"Where's Kat?"

Katrina. The mere mention of her name in any form makes my stomach churn. She's been out of sight, out of mind. The memory of her showing up at my lunch with Blake back in January and shredding his wife Jen storms into my head. The alcohol burns through my blood as my cheeks heat up.

"She's couldn't come." My voice wavers. "She had previous commitments."

Blake takes another swig of his drink and nods. "That's good, man."

What does he mean? At our lunch, I remember his icy hostility toward Katrina. It bordered on rage as Katrina's out of control behavior became audacious. Mortifying. It was obvious to me they had some kind of history, but Blake was tight-lipped about it. And I chose not to pursue it further. When I confronted Katrina about her outrageous behavior and their past, she told me Blake, the former love of her life, had broken her heart. I left it at that, never questioning it further.

Loosened up by the Scotch, I build up the courage to prod. His tumbler half emptied, maybe he'll open up and tell me more.

"Blake, what happened between you and Kat?" I deliberately use the name he calls her.

He drains the rest of his Scotch and sets the glass on the table between us. His blustery blue eyes meet mine. "Listen, Brandon, I can't go into details, but that girl is bad news."

Rather than unnerving me, his pronouncement affirms what I already know and gives me the impetus to probe further.

"What do you mean?"

"She's capable of a lot of shit. I'll leave it at that. Hey, man, I shouldn't be telling you this stuff. You're marrying her. Maybe she's different with you and has found what she needs."

I blurt out the next words. "Blake, I'm going to be honest with you. I'm having second thoughts about marrying her." I don't tell him that I attempted to break up with her before this trip, but she left town and I couldn't reach her on her cell. Probably because there's no reception at her father's high security penitentiary.

Blake twists his lips, forming a less than happy expression. Judging by the look on his face, maybe it was meant to be that I couldn't get in touch with Katrina. After being around her, I can only imagine what kind of damage she would do me in the press while I'm half way around the world at MIP. I inwardly shudder. Drawing in a sharp breath, production chief Blake finally breaks his silence and confirms my unsettling gut feelings.

"I wish you'd said something to me or our Press Department earlier. Our research shows that viewers are as excited about your televised wedding as much as they are for the *Kurt Kussler* season finale. You—or should I say we—have a lot riding on both events. And Katrina's a loose cannon, the proverbial wrecking ball, and ready to blow everything up. Man, I honestly don't know what to say. The timing sucks for a breakup."

Christ. What have I gotten myself into? I'm damned if I do; damned if I don't. A sudden bout of turbulence shakes the plane and cuts our conversation short. The clamor of clattering glasses sounds in my ears as the "Fasten Seatbelts" sign flashes overhead. I shift my gaze to my adorable assistant who's talking to Blake's wife Jennifer to make sure she's alright. She's looks a little terrified. I fight the urge to jump up from my seat and take her in my arms. Blake catches my eyes on her.

"Your assistant's great," he comments. "She's really cute too."

"Yeah, she is," I mumble under my breath, wondering if Blake suspects something.

The turbulence fortunately doesn't last long. But the shaky feeling inside me doesn't go away as the air calms down. Blake undoes his seatbelt and asks an attendant to refill our glasses. After the attractive woman accommodates us, he takes another gulp of his Scotch and then sets the tumbler down on his muscular thighs. With his tall athletic build and movie-star looks, we could practically be brothers.

"Brandon, I've been thinking about what you told me. Do what you need to do. My wise old man always says no risk, no gain."

Tugging at my lower lip, I digest his father's words of wisdom. The stakes are high. I have everything to gain… and everything to lose. Why do I feel like a smooth ride is not in my cards?

Chapter 19

Zoey

From the corner of my eye, I catch Brandon returning to his seat. His eyes lock on me, and he gestures for me to return to mine. Boss's orders. Chat time is over. I excuse myself, but not before Jen gives me a hug. I really like her and have a good feeling we may become close friends as Jeffrey and Chaz's wedding plans unfold.

"What were you and Jennifer Burns talking about?" asks Brandon as I plop back down on the roomy leather chair.

Mr. Nosy. "Stuff."

"What kind of stuff?"

"Girl stuff. And what about you and Blake? You two looked intense."

"Business. We talked mostly about MIP. I have a full day on the floor tomorrow. And there's going to be a Q&A session after the screening tomorrow night. I'm going to need you to help me prepare for it."

"Sure, no prob." I have to remind myself this is a business trip. My James Bond-inspired dreams of tooling around the French Riviera and Monaco fly out the window. I'm back to being his go-to assistant.

Over a scrumptious dinner of beef bourguignon and free-flowing wine and champagne, Brandon and I review his hectic schedule. Every minute of the next few days is jam-packed with events and meetings. I get exhausted just thinking about it. Somewhere between my third glass of champagne and dessert, my eyes grow heavy. I doze off.

"Ladies and gentlemen, please return your seats to an upright position and fasten your seatbelts in preparation for landing. We will be arriving at Nice International Airport in approximately fifteen minutes."

At the sound of the announcement, I snap open my eyes. Mortification sweeps through me. I fell asleep with my head resting on Brandon's strong shoulder, my cheek brushing his mountainous bicep. Straightening, I glance down at my watch. We've been in the air for over twelve hours. The time in Nice is seven p.m.

"Hi," I squeak, totally embarrassed. I must look all sleepy-faced.

"Hi," he says back with a dazzling smile. He tucks a few strands of hair that have fallen into my eye behind my ear, bringing awareness back into my body, and then buckles my seatbelt for me, an endearing gesture that sends tingles to my core. "Are you excited?"

"Yes, very," I say breathily as I look down at the mesmerizing view of the Mediterranean below us.

"Me too."

In more ways than one. Another view takes my breath away—the prominent bulge that dominates the area between his legs. His enormous cock is straining against his jeans. Maybe he fell asleep too and had a wet dream? I can't get my eyes off his fly knowing what lies beneath. I feel myself flushing as a fresh rush of flutters pulses through me.

"Are you okay?" asks Brandon.

I quickly shift my vision to his gorgeous face. His thick-lashed violet eyes penetrate me and a knowing smirk curls his luscious lips.

"Um, uh, I'm a little nervous about the plane landing."

He playfully flicks my nose. "Don't worry. The equipment's fine. It's going to go down as smoothly as it went up. It just may take a little longer."

"Oh," I spout, reading way too much into his words. Heat blossoms between my legs, visualizing his cockpit. Squeezing my thighs together, I take a deep, calming breath.

Sure enough, we land without a hitch. An imposing stretch limo meets our aircraft on the tarmac to transport us to The Carlton Hotel where we're all staying. While the gang files into the car, my eyes stay on Brandon as he zips open a classy, monogrammed satchel and pulls out his leather bomber jacket and another similar smaller sized one. He hands the latter to me.

"Here. Put this on. You're going to need it."

While breezy, it's mild, and I'm perfectly fine in the short-sleeved jersey top I'm wearing. I protest.

"For fuck's sake, just do it." God, he's bossy.

Without questioning him, I do as I'm told. I zip up the very hip jacket which inside bears Chaz's label. Brandon secretly purchased it? It fits me perfectly and the leather feels buttery against my skin.

After donning his jacket, Brandon ushers me into the limo and then joins me. He tells the driver to make a stop at Platinum. A disco? I'm confused.

I'm even more confused when the driver pulls up to a car rental agency just outside the airport.

"Zoey, this is where we get out."

"Huh? Aren't we going to The Carlton too?"

"Yup." He bids farewell to our companions. "We'll catch up with you guys later."

The chauffeur exits the car and comes around it to open the passenger door. Brandon steps out and then grabs my hand to help me out. He asks the driver to drop off our luggage at the hotel and hands him a generous tip.

Holding my hand, he leads me inside the car rental

place.

"Zoey, have you ever ridden a bike?"

Jesus. We're going to bike into Cannes? Pedal down some scenic path along the Mediterranean? Oh shit. It's like a sixteen-mile ride. I don't know if I'm up for that. Brandon breaks into my mini panic attack.

"Answer me, Zoey. Yes or no?"

My hand grows clammy in his. I gulp. "Yes. I had a two-wheeler."

Brandon bursts into hysterical laughter. "Oh, Zoey, Zoey, Zoey. You're too fucking adorable."

"Are you mocking me?"

Still roaring with laughter, Brandon marches us up to the rental counter.

Well, naïve me is in for a big surprise. Fifteen short minutes later, my big butt's on a bike all right. A sleek violet Ducati Monster Bike—a muscular, coiled, ready for action, sexy beast—just like Brandon. My thighs clench the back seat and my arms clutch his waist as we weave in and out of the insane traffic along the Mediterranean.

"Brandon, you're going to get us killed!" I shriek, holding on to him for dear life.

"Zoey, there's no need to shout. I can hear you just fine."

The clarity of his voice inside my helmet is shocking. "There's a microphone in here?"

"Yup. Now chill and enjoy the ride."

"But, Brandon. Why couldn't you just rent a car?"

"Because this is much faster. Easy to park. And way more fun. Plus with these tinted helmets, no one will recognize us, including the paparazzi."

He makes good points. Especially the last one. Ahead of us, an accident is cleared from the road and the bumper-to-bumper traffic eases up.

"Hold on tight." Brandon squeezes the throttle.

V-room! On my next breath, we're zooming down the scenic N98 at over a hundred miles per hour. My heart's racing at about the same speed. I try not to scream since he can hear me. Instead, I lean in and cling to him, so tightly I can feel the planes and angles of his taut six-pack beneath his sinfully sexy jacket.

The speed is not the only thing that's driving me to squeal. The vibration of the roaring motor is stimulating my clit. And the glorious sensation between my thighs is compounded by the fact that my mound's rubbing against his gorgeous ass. Wetness mixes with sparks of pure bliss.

"Are you enjoying the ride now?" I hear him ask.

"Oh yes!" I say breathlessly. The warm air whips under my clothes, and the delicious sensation between my legs permeates every cell. And the truth is I'm finally relaxed enough to soak in the orgasmic view.

I'm blown away by the scenery. It's spectacular. On one side of the dusk-lit road, the cerulean Mediterranean laps the rock-filled shoreline while on the other, pastel-colored villas dot flowering hills. It kind of reminds me of Malibu, but it's ten times more beautiful. For a brief minute, I work up the courage to lift my visor with one hand and inhale deeply through my nose. The air smells divine. A heady blend of lavender and the sea mixes with the intoxicating scent of Brandon's leather jacket.

Brandon expertly maneuvers the sleek motorcycle as if he were born to ride it. He removes one of his hands from the handlebar and slips it under his helmet. A sudden blast of techno music fills my ears—stuff I would never listen to at home, but I like it. It feels right. Makes me exhilarated.

"Are you okay?" Brandon shouts above the thudding music.

"More than okay," I shout back. I feel like I'm stoned. On a high. I truly can't believe I'm here in the South of France with Brandon Taylor. The hottest man on the planet. Attending the gala world premiere of the season finale of *Kurt Kussler*. Pinch me again. No, don't bother.

"Do you like this bike?"

"I love it! Does it shoot missiles and lasers?" Seriously, it's the Aston Martin of motorcycles, and in my head, I imagine Brandon as James Bond driving a decked out one.

Brandon laughs. "No. But maybe the one I'm going to buy will. I need to protect you."

A shudder runs through me. For the first time in days, I think about Donatelli. There's no way he can be anywhere here in France. I quickly shove his ugly face to the back of mind and refocus my attention on Brandon.

"You're really going to buy a Ducati?"

"Yup."

"You're going to have to annex your garage."

"Nah. I'm going to get rid of the Lambo. Been there, done that."

I wish he would dump the Hummer. The memory of driving the monster flashes into my head. *Not. Good.* I've lost count of how many times I crashed it. I sure as hell hope Brandon doesn't make me drive this beast with him on the back seat.

As if reading my mind, he gives my thigh a little squeeze. "Don't worry, Zo. You're never going to touch this baby."

I mentally sigh with relief and go back to enjoying my Bond-girl ride. Along the way, Brandon points out several sights, including Nice's iconic Negresco Hotel, and later on, Gregory Peck's former majestic villa, and as we enter Cannes, a sign saying: "Cannes: Sister City to Beverly Hills." There's one just like it on Santa Monica Boulevard; I've passed it countless times.

"You remember being here before?" I ask him as we drive past the famous sign. He was actually here last Spring, a trip I helped plan.

"Yeah. Totally. I know this area like the back of my hand."

Lately, he's been having a lot of memory break-throughs. I wonder if he's remembered anything more about the day of his accident. I'm dying to ask him, but don't want to break this euphoria with dark thoughts. Instead, I just let myself enjoy the scenery, the music, and my breathtaking companion. Timeless beauty comes in many forms—be it a magnificent landscape, a high-powered bike, or a panty-melting man.

The Carlton is Cannes's grand dame of hotels. I'm in awe of it as we bypass a line of limos and pull up to the paparazzi-swarmed entrance. Built in 1911, it's a sand-colored palace in the center of La Croisette, the busy palm tree-lined boulevard across from the Mediterranean. Its big claim to fame is that it was prominently featured in *To Catch a Thief*, starring Grace Kelly and Cary Grant, one of my favorite movies, and where the actress later met her future husband, Prince Rainier of Monaco.

"Keep your helmet on," Brandon says as he scoots off the bike. Balancing it, he gives a hard kick to the kickstand while I dismount.

It's far from a graceful move, and I'm not standing steady. From squeezing the Ducati so hard, my legs are like Jell-O. And to top it off, my clit's still throbbing. I'm not sure if I can walk. I take a step and I wobble. While I can't see Brandon's expression beneath his tinted helmet, I can feel his smirk on me. *Cocky jerk!*

A valet jogs up to us. Extending his thumb and forefinger, Brandon makes his signature *Kurt Kussler* finger gun gesture and aims it at the man. With a big smile, the uniformed attendant responds with recognition written on his face.

"Get *eet*. Got *eet?* Good... *Bienvenue,* Monsieur Taylor."

"It's good to be back, Alec," replies Brandon, handing him a substantial tip in Euros. His memory has indeed come back.

Taking me by the crook of my arm, Brandon brushes past the smarmy paparazzi, who don't recognize him, and escorts me into the bustling hotel lobby to check in. I take in my surroundings. There's a large bar and a restaurant, decorated in opulent Belle Époque furnishings and filled with beautiful bronzed movers and shakers. I recognize some stars from other TV shows, but none of them are as big as Brandon. The chic woman at the check-in counter also recognizes Brandon despite the fact he's incognito and is equally happy to see him. I shudder thinking how close he came to not making it back here and wonder again if he's recalled anything about his accident. I'm sure he'd tell me as well as Pops.

There's no need to leave credit cards or passports as Conquest Broadcasting has handled everything. We're told our bags are already in our rooms. My room is a single on the fifth floor while Brandon's got one of the movie star penthouse suites two floors above me. The Sean Connery suite, named after Brandon's idol because that's where he's often stayed. How fitting! Brandon drops me off at my room and flips me around before I can insert my key card. His hipbones dig into me, pressing me tight against the door. He's dangerously close to me, his hardness grazing my middle.

He unfastens the buckle of my chinstrap, his fingers brushing the sensitive crook of my neck. It must be one of my erogenous zones because flutters go flying to my core, igniting a fire between my thighs.

Rather than taking off the helmet, he lifts up the tinted faceplate and then does the same with his. We're a whisper away. His warm breath skims my exposed flesh. A hot tingle spirals through me like an uncoiled spring.

"Do you feel jet lagged?" he breathes into my parted lips.

"No, I feel great." Is he kidding? I feel more than great. Totally exhilarated and turned on. Every cell in my body is buzzing with need and desire.

His smoldering violet eyes bore into me. They're radiating heat on my cheeks. I feel myself flushing. Growing weak in the knees.

"Good. I want to take you out for dinner. I know a great little place in The Old Town overlooking Le Vieux Port that the paparazzi don't know about. We can sneak out the back way."

"Sure." I can barely manage the word. "What should I wear?"

He smiles seductively. "Any dress that has a zipper."

"Are we biking there?" I ask, running my memory through my new acquisitions for something that'll let me straddle my legs. The pickings are slim. Most of my new Chaz wardrobe is skintight.

"I'm not sure."

He releases me, and I turn to insert the card into the key slot. My fingers quivering, I have to slide it in and out several times before the door unlocks. I can feel his amused smirk on me.

"I'll pick you up at eight thirty. Be ready." His tone is bossy.

"I will be." Without saying another word, I slam the door behind me and, after catching my breath, bang my helmeted head against the slab of wood. So hard I could have knocked myself out had it not been for the protective gear. I remain plastered against the door like a shell-shocked zombie. Holy shit! Did Brandon Taylor just ask me out on a date? My heart is about to beat out of my chest and ricochet straight through my leather bomber jacket. I try to contain and convince myself it's just a business dinner to go over his MIP schedule, but it's impossible.

The enchanting restaurant Brandon takes me to is located across from the water in Le Suquet, Cannes's "Old Town." To avoid paparazzi and fanfare, we rode the Ducati here though it's just a short fifteen-minute walk from The Carlton. The spiffy bike is parked on the street just outside the restaurant.

It feels like a whole different world. Unlike the glitzy hotel-lined part of the Croisette, charming stone and stucco houses line the hillside terrain along with a towering medieval church. The restaurant overlooks the picturesque harbor. Soft laps of the Mediterranean sound in my ears and boat lights brighten the starry sky. There's only one word for the setting—romantic.

"You look really nice," Brandon comments as we wait to be seated. "That dress becomes you."

With a flush of goosebumps, I smile and thank him for the compliment. I'm wearing one of Chaz's sexy creations—a slenderizing strapless black high-low number. The flowy skirt with its asymmetrical layers of chiffon made it easy for me to straddle my legs on the Ducati. Thank goodness, it was such a short ride because the rest of my outfit was far from ideal—you try sitting on your ass on the back of a motorcycle with strappy stilettos and scanty lace panties. There are wedgies and there *are* wedgies. But I survived. And I'm grateful my hair survived the helmet. Loose, it falls over my shoulders in soft waves and complements the extra make-up I'm wearing.

I have to admit I look and feel like a million bucks. Glamorous enough to be seen with the likes of Brandon Taylor. I soak him in. Holy hotness! He looks devastating, dressed in a free-fitting collarless lavender linen shirt that he's left partly unbuttoned… relaxed faded jeans… and a pair of expensive Italian black loafers. Of course, no socks. The epitome of pure movie star effortless sexiness. Despite the light breeze, heat spirals from my knees to my core.

"Ah! Great! Here comes Antoine," my gorgeous companion says brightly, sparing me from saying something stupid or trite.

A wide grin stretches across the maître-d's face upon setting his eyes on Brandon. A robust man with a jet-black handlebar mustache, he gives him a kiss on each cheek.

"Monsieur Taylor, it *eez* so good to see you again! *Comment ça-va?*"

"*Très bien*, Antoine." He must also be the owner as the restaurant is called Antoine's.

"*Fantastique*. You gave my wife *et moi* a great scare with *zee* accident."

"I'm fine now," Brandon assures him. "Perfectly fine."

Smiling, the relieved Frenchman shifts his attention to me. "And who *eez* this beau-tee-ful woman? A girlfriend, *peut-être?*"

Brandon laces his fingers with mine. "She's more than a girlfriend."

A shiver skitters down my spine at both his unexpected gesture and words. What does he mean by that? Before I can manage a word, Antoine asks us where we prefer to sit. While it's only mid-April, the balmy weather is summer-like, easily in the seventies. Brandon chooses a corner table for two outside overlooking the port. We pass a table occupied by a teenage couple goo-goo eyed in love and then several older locals engaged in lively conversation until catching sight of Brandon. Everywhere he goes, he turns heads, whether they recognize him or not. Unleashing my hand, my breathtaking companion helps me into a wicker bistro chair before lowering himself onto one facing me. The table is covered with a red-checkered tablecloth and is candlelit. The flickering candle bathes Brandon's face in a warm glow, making him appear ethereal. Like a god. With his smoldering violet eyes and lashes so thick they should be illegal, that spiky muss of onyx hair, a parted mouth made for kissing... and let's not forget that sculpted body... can anyone be more ridiculously beautiful? I'm glad I'm sitting because every bone in my body is liquid.

"Can I get you some apéritifs?" asks Antoine.

Brandon answers. "*Oui.* Two Americanos."

"*Parfait.* I shall be right back." Antoine scurries

off.

I crinkle my nose. "Brandon, you've ordered Star-bucks coffees?" An iced Americano is his morning brew of choice and a hot version mine.

Brandon laughs. "No, Zoey. It's the original James Bond cocktail. It's made with Campari, vermouth, and soda water. Antoine makes them with Perrier just the way 007 prefers them."

"Oh." A small voice inside my head tells me I shouldn't be drinking. It *is* a business dinner, *right?*

"Trust me, you'll like it."

"I think I'm going to pass."

"Stop it. I want you to try it."

The drinks come in no time. "Let's toast," says Brandon, his eyes twinkling.

"Sure." Falling under his spell, it takes all my effort to utter one little word. My vocabulary has grown limited.

"To us," Brandon says demonstratively and then we clink our tumblers. The sparkling glasses ping like a bell. I follow Brandon and take a sip of the vibrant red cocktail.

"What do you think?" he asks.

I digest the flavor and swallow hard. The aftertaste is so bitter it makes my toes curl.

"I like it," I say, screwing up my face.

Brandon leans into me and dusts my contorted lips with his forefinger. "You're so adorable when you lie."

Uh oh! He's caught me in the act. That fateful spanking flashes into my head. He told me never to lie to him again. I could be in big trouble. Yet, I'm strangely excited in a good way.

His fingertip trails down the side of my face. He traces my jaw until he lands on the tip of my chin. Making little circles, he lets out a sexy laugh. "Don't worry about it. Campari is an acquired taste."

"I'll get used to it," I say and bravely take another sip. The liquor courses down my throat and into my bloodstream, warming me. You know what? It's not so bad after all.

Antoine brings us two menus. Brandon orders for the both of us, choosing the house special—fresh mussels meuniere and a side of frites (which I learn are French Fries) plus a bottle of wine—a local Rosé from Provence. I take a few more sips of the Campari cocktail, the potent alcohol loosening me up.

"The view is spectacular," I quip.

"It is," agrees Brandon, eyeing my cleavage, which is prominently displayed by the body-hugging bodice of my dress. I cross my legs under the table and pretend I don't notice.

"Who do all those boats belong to?" While we passed monstrous yachts docked outside the majestic Palais des Festivals where MIP is taking place, the vessels here are much smaller and hardly pretentious.

Brandon finishes his Americano and sets the apéritif

glass down. "Those are fisherman boats. Before Cannes became a center for Hollywood glitz and glamour, it used to be a small fishing village. Fishermen still make a living here. Many sell to local restaurateurs, including Antoine, who I'm sure got the mussels we ordered straight off a boat today."

I take another hit of the Campari cocktail. "Have you ever gone swimming in the Mediterranean?"

He smiles. "Dozens of times. The water is incredible. If we have time, I want to take you swimming."

A frisson of anxiety curls in my gut. Not only am I afraid of swimming in the sea, but I also sure as hell don't want Brandon to see me in a bathing suit again.

"I don't think so. You know, I'm still afraid of the ocean."

He laughs. "The Mediterranean isn't an ocean. It's a sea. And technically, the part here in Cannes is a bay. So, the water is very calm. Barely a wave."

"B-but I didn't bring a bathing suit." The truth. I never even thought of bringing one since I packed so hastily.

He laughs again and unnerves me. "Don't worry about it. I'll buy you a bikini."

I gulp. A bikini—the last thing I want to be caught dead in! Especially with Brandon. As I envision the worst, he continues.

"There's probably a boutique right in the hotel." He regards me coyly. "You may only need a bottom. Most women here sun and swim topless."

I gulp again. The ring of Brandon's phone saves me from responding. Thank God, because I'm at a loss for words.

My eyes stay on him as he pulls out his cell from his jeans pocket and glances down at the caller ID. His lips twist and his brows furrow. Katrina? The phone continues to ring while I anxiously circle the rim of my glass with my fingertip. To my relief, he doesn't answer it, and, in fact, turns it off. "Fuck it," he mumbles under his breath. His frown morphs into a smile when Antoine personally brings us our meal along with the bottle of wine.

"Bon appetit," says the jovial man, setting our order down.

The tantalizing, garlicky aroma of the mussels wafts up my nose. My appetite is aroused.

"Antoine makes the best mussels meuniere in all of the Riviera," Brandon tells me.

Antoine smiles proudly. He uncorks the wine and pours Brandon a bit. Brandon takes a sip and nods approvingly. *"C'est parfait."*

It's perfect. He's perfect. We share the big bowl of mussels and the crispy fries, sensuously feeding helpings to one another and imbibing the refreshing pink wine between bites. Moans escape my mouth. Not only are the mussels divine, but their tender meat is also charging me with sexual energy. Mussels must be some kind of aphrodisiac. But actually, everything is turning me on. The food, the wine, the setting. And most of all, the mouth-watering man sitting across from me. My eyes don't waver from him as I feed him the last mussel. His luscious lips clamp down on the edible part and then he sucks on it.

"Mmm," he moans, closing his eyes as he does. Every ounce of me is buzzing and there's a wet fire inside my panties. He swallows and licks his upper lip. Another gush of wetness and a rush of hot tingles besiege me. He re-opens his eyes and meets my gaze, holding it fiercely. Before either of us can say word, a staunch, swarthy woman appears on the terrace. Holding an accordion, she heads our way. Once at our table, she stretches out the instrument and starts to serenade us.

"Inoubliable ..."

Oh my God! In one word, the song is instantly recognizable. "Unforgettable." Mama's favorite song ... sung in French. With the husky voice of a fallen angel, the songstress's moving rendition pulls at my heartstrings. Tears flood my eyes.

"Why are you crying?" Brandon asks, tenderly brushing my unstoppable tears away.

"This was Mama's favorite song. She sang it all the time. It reminded her of Papa." Sniffling, I pause while the dark memory fills my head. "It was playing on the Pier when she was shot."

"I'm sorry. It's a beautiful song," he says softly, cutting into the painful, unforgettable memory. His violet eyes burn right through me and his voice grows softer. "Almost as beautiful as you."

My watering eyes blink several times while my breath hitches in my throat and my heart hammers against my chest. His words swirl around in my head like confetti. They shower my flesh with flecks of heightened sensation and my soul with explosive emotion. I begin to unravel.

And then he does something that totally turns me into vapor. Tracing my tear-soaked jaw, Brandon sings along in English, his voice pure velvet, as devastating as the man he is.

"Oh, Brandon!" I weep out his name. The impact of this magical moment has reduced me to mush.

Still singing and melting my heart, my gorgeous god of a man stands up, and rounding the table, pulls out my chair. "Dance with me, Zoey." A soft but strong command.

On my next sniffle, I'm in his strong arms, my head resting on his beating heart, my arms draped around his shoulders, as he moves me slowly to the melody and words. Swaying me side to side, he sings into my ear while tears stream down my face and dampen his linen shirt. I lose myself in him with each slow measured step. It's as if there is no one else in the world but the two of us. *Unforgettable...* as the word drifts into a hypnotic hum, he draws me closer to him, pressing his lips on my scalp. I feel the warmth of them and his taut body flush against mine. I melt into his ripples and his arousal. He owns me and I don't have the strength or desire to break away. Physically or mentally.

I'm drunk with emotion. And one forbidden four-letter word. So intoxicated, I can't think straight or question what I'm doing. I just cling to him. Like a song of love. Finally, I lift my head, and look up at him, my misty eyes searching for answers. His impassioned gaze holds me captive. My already racing pulse accelerates.

"Brandon—" I don't know what words will spill out of my mouth next, if any at all. It doesn't matter. Because on my next heartbeat, he fists my hair and tugs back my head. Before I can take another breath, his lips come crashing down on mine like a meteor. Still humming, he sucks and gnaws my hungry mouth. White-hot balls of passion explode inside me, showering me with fireworks from my head to my toes. I moan into his mouth and then I part my lips, allowing his tongue to find mine. Entwined, our tongues dance sensuously, swirling and twirling to the music and lyrics. Oh my God. This kiss! This incredible kiss! I cup his strong, stubbled jaw, deepening, and extending it, as he draws me closer, one hand gripping my ass. The song drifts into my ears like a magic carpet. The sparks now blind me. I squeeze my eyes shut. Yet, he's all I see. Never before has anyone been so unforgettable in every way. After what seems like an eternity, the timeless song ends, and he gently breaks his lips away. My heavy eyelids rise like theater curtains, and our glazed eyes lock in a passionate exchange. Shouts of "bravo" from patrons and bystanders reverberate in my ears. I feel myself flush with embarrassment, but Brandon's dimpled smile fills me with a rush of lust and desire as he holds me tight in his arms.

Tears flow from my eyes. Everything's been so perfect. The setting. The meal. Our dance. Our kiss. But something is so wrong with this picture. A blaring ambulance races by. The sound of the siren startles me back to my senses, out of my drunken stupor. Brandon's name burns on my heart. Remorse singes my brain. I want to rip that dazzling smile off his face. What the hell is he doing? What the hell am I doing? As reality sets in, so does a bitter mix of panic and regret.

Oblivious, Brandon kisses my tears away and then breathes against my neck. "Baby, let's make this night *unforgettable.*"

Chapter 20

Brandon

She clings to me like I'm her lifeline while her tears soak my shirt. This unexpected serenade has changed everything. It's made her vulnerable. And it's made me vulnerable. Zoey is special and she's fragile. I'm suddenly afraid of hurting her. The giddy flirtation we shared over dinner has dissipated into the night air. Dancing with her to this song has done things to me I've never experienced before. Everything I'm feeling is for real. This is not Brandon the actor. This is Brandon the man. A man I've never known nor can I remember. A hopeless romantic. I mapped out the evening—sharing a nice dinner, getting a little drunk, then heading back to the hotel and fucking her senseless. But now, my need to love her trumps my need to fuck her. I want to hold her. Caress her. Taste her. Get to know every bit of her. Pleasure her every way I can.

Emotionally charged, I make a quick run to the men's room. When I return to the table, she's gone. My eyes dart around the restaurant, but she's nowhere in sight. Maybe she went to the ladies' room?

Antoine ambles over to the table with the check.

"Antoine, have you seen … my friend?" I ask. *What do I call her?*

"Ah, Monsieur Taylor. She ran out of *zee* restaurant. Very upset. *Eez* everything okay?"

Fuck. No. I quickly look at the bill and throw two hundred Euros on the table. Way more than the cost of the dinner, but I don't have time to wait for the change. I thank Antoine and sprint out of the restaurant.

Shit. Which way did she go? Instinctively, I guess east, thinking she may be heading back to the hotel. She couldn't have gotten too far in her heels.

I hop on the bike and rev it up. Without bothering to put on my helmet, which is dangling with Zoey's from the handlebar, I charge down the sidewalk, full throttle, weaving in and out of stunned pedestrians. The motor roars in my ears right along with my apprehension.

"Attention!" I shout out in French when what I want to shout is get the fuck out of my way. Angry promenaders shout back what I believe are French expletives. I deserve every one.

Yes, I am a crazy asshole. I'm not in my right mind. But right now desperation is negating any form of sanity. I have to find her. How far could she have gotten? Cranking my head to the left to look up an alley, I face forward again and freak. Fuck. I'm going to run into a gay couple strolling hand in hand in front of me. Plugged into their iPhones, they don't hear me behind them.

"Watch out!" I scream at the top of my lungs as I squeeze the brake lever.

"What the fuck are you doing, you crazy American?" shouts one of the dudes, yanking his partner to safety just in the nick of time. Losing control of the Ducati, I go flying—*Crash!*—and smash into a kiosk. My heart thudding, I drop my feet to the ground to steady the smoking bike and then hop off it. It tumbles to the pavement with a clang.

Fuck the bike. Without wasting a second, I dash down the Croisette, almost knocking down a few more people. I'm surprised I still don't see her. Shit. Maybe she turned up one of Old Town's winding streets. I'll never find her.

About to give up hope, I finally spot her. She's running barefoot about one hundred yards ahead of me. The long, flowy skirt of her dress billows like a sail.

"Zoey!" I shout out, running after her at breakneck speed.

She doesn't stop or look back. Picking up her pace, she turns up one of the serpentine streets off the Croisette. I'm not going to lose her.

I pick up speed, running so fast my lungs and thighs

are on fire. I may be a swimmer, but sprinting's not my thing. Breathing heavily, I turn up the narrow street and see her. She's within shouting distance.

"Zoey!" I cry out again.

"Leave me alone!" Her sobbing is gutting me.

Calling on all the muscle power I have, I jet-propel myself up the steep, winding cobblestone street. With me hot on her trail, she turns down a very narrow alley. It's dark and deserted, lined by neighborhood grocery stores all closed till morning. She's slowing. I'm so close I can taste her. Finally, I catch up to her and, cinching her waist, stop her in her tracks.

"Go away!" she cries, her sobs mixing with pants. She fights me off like a captured wild animal, writhing, and kicking, but even in my breathless state, she's no match for my strength. In one swift move, I flip her around by her shoulders and walk her backward until she's flattened against one of the storefronts. A boulangerie. I lift her arms high above her head and hold them tight against the rough stucco wall. My weight presses against her so she can't free herself. She's my prisoner. My prey.

"Let me go!" She squirms, angry tears streaming down her face.

"I will once you tell me why you ran away from me." Rage fuels my voice.

"What kind of sicko game are you playing with me, Brandon?"

"What do you mean?" My voice is a little softer.

"You're fucking engaged to Katrina, almost about to marry her, and you're coming on to me?"

I draw in a sharp breath and let out a loud huff. "We need to talk."

Her stormy eyes search mine for answers.

"Zoey, it's complicated."

"Isn't that a convenient word?" Sniveling, she turns her head away.

"Look at me, Zoey."

She refuses. She's so fucking stubborn.

"Zoey, did you hear me? Look at me!"

Slowly, she turns her head. Our eyes lock.

"I'm having second thoughts about Katrina."

"What do you mean?" she asks, repeating my earlier words.

"I don't love her. I don't even like her."

Her teary eyes flutter, and I can feel her heart pounding against my chest as I rattle on.

"I still can't remember shit about our relationship. Whatever I had with her before my accident, I have no longer. I can't even stand fucking her."

Zoey's eyes narrow as her lips purse. "If my memory serves me correctly, you sure seemed to be getting off on her when I caught you with your dick down her throat."

I snicker. "Well, your precious memory is wrong. She seduced me; it wasn't by choice. And I was groaning because she bit me. I couldn't even get it up."

A little smile curls on Zoey's kissable lips. Good. A turning point. Because the hard part is coming. Again, no pun intended. I've got to talk about my feelings. Something I've never done with anyone, with the exception of my mentor.

"Zoey." I take a long pause after saying her name. "I have feelings for someone else."

"Oh, some other actress? Or 'it girl'?"

"Jesus, Zoey. Don't you know?"

She's making it so fucking hard for me. Literally, in more ways than one. My aching cock is straining against my fly, about to burst through at any moment. I want her so badly.

One word: "You."

Her jaw drops open. One word back: "Oh."

Okay. I've said it. The words get easier for me. "I brought you here to spend time with you. Away from LA. Away from Katrina. I want to know if the connection I feel with you is real. You've aroused sensations and emotions I've never felt before."

"How can you be sure with your amnesia?" she challenges, looking deep into my eyes.

"I'm sure. I remember everything about the last ten years except the accident and the month leading up to it. And I remember you touched something inside me the minute I met you. You were adorable. I wanted to spread your legs and take you on my driveway in the pouring rain."

"Really?" Her voice is so small she might as well be speechless.

Here goes. Maybe I should have written a soliloquy and rehearsed it. I suck at ad-libbing. I always have.

"Zo, my memory's come back, but I've been losing my mind over you. That night you went out with your brother, I went berserk with fear and jealousy. I thought I was going to lose you... that you were the one he was getting engaged to. That's why I followed you to Fig & Olive. I was going to stop him even if I had to do something I'd later regret doing. You brought something out in me that my amnesia suppressed. Perhaps something I've *always* suppressed. My need for you. My need to dominate you. My need to possess you. My need to protect you. When I found out about your little charade, I totally lost control. Then, after I spanked you, I couldn't get you out of my system. All I could think about was making you mine. But you ran away from me. I thought I'd lost you forever. Those seven... ten... twelve... whatever days were the darkest, most unbearable days of my life."

Zoey's big brown eyes stay riveted on me. They hardly blink. The words pour out of me as if I'm thinking out loud.

"Zoey, all of me wants all of you. I can have any woman I want, but I only want you. You understand me. Accept me for who I am. You make me laugh and feel alive. When you're with me, I'm whole. When you're away from me, I lose control. I fall apart. I don't function. All I do is fantasize about you. You're a fucking pain in my ass, but you fucking turn me on. Drive me crazy. And don't tell me you don't feel something toward me. Actions speak louder than words. I'm an actor. An observer. I've watched you carefully over the last few months. Make that few years. You've wanted me as much as I've wanted you. When I kissed you tonight, you deepened it, totally succumbed with your body and soul."

"B-but—"

I cut her off. "My beautiful Zoey, I know this is all wrong. And in the back of my mind, know that cheating on the woman I'm engaged to will come back to bite me in the ass, but I want you so badly I'd chase you around the world. I'd even kill for you."

Soft whimpers escape her quivering lips. Her chest heaves against mine.

"What's the matter, my beauty?" I ask softly as another round of tears pours down her face. I kiss them away.

"Oh, Brandon. I know this is wrong too. So crazy wrong. But I want you to take me. Right now. Right here. Please. I want you to fuck me."

"Oh, baby, you don't know *how* much I want you." I'm going to lose my mind again if I can't have her on my next breath. I smother her mouth with mine to suppress her sobs. Releasing her hands, I yank open my belt buckle, fumble with my jeans button, and then unzip my fly. My cock is rock-hard, aching to be inside her. I dip my hand into my jeans pocket.

"Put this on me," I command, handing her the foiled condom package.

With trembling fingers, she rips it open and rolls the latex along the thick length of my throbbing shaft. I hiss at her touch. Condom in place, I shove up her little dress and yank down her scanty lace panties. Damn. I should have just ripped them off I think as she wastes time stepping out of them.

Panties off, I reward her with another hot kiss. With our mouths connected and our tongues entwined, I lift her up against the wall by her haunches. Instinctively, she folds her arms around my neck and her legs around my hips. My hands grip her delicious ass. We're perfectly lined up. Face to face. Heart to Heart. Organ to Organ. I break the long kiss.

"Baby, I want you to put my cock inside you. I need to feel those magical fingers around it." I squeeze her ass. "Don't worry, I've got you."

Nodding feverishly, she unfolds one of her arms from my shoulders and lowering it, curls those long, slender fingers around my erection at the base. She applies pressure and I groan. So help me God. So fucking good. Gripping it, she puts the wide tip to her fiery clit, rubbing it against her slickness. I groan again.

Then, inch by thick inch, she slides my cock inside her. I hiss again. Christ. She's so hot. So wet. So tight. She takes me to the hilt and I curse under my breath.

She moans.

"Are you okay, baby?" I ask with concern. I'm so big I could rip her apart.

"Oh, Brandon. You feel so good."

"The same. Your beautiful pussy was made for me." With a grunt, I push into her and then slide my cock back down. And then I thrust my length back into her.

"Aah." She digs her fingernails into my shoulder blades.

"My beauty, I'm going to give you a fucking you'll never forget. I'm going to fuck you fast. I'm going to fuck you hard. So hard, you'll be headed to the moon. If you can't take it, let me know. Do you remember your safe word?"

Biting down on her lip, she nods.

A couple more long, slow strokes and then I pummel her.

Clutching my shoulders, she holds on for the ride of her life. I can't believe how natural it feels to fuck her. My cock is in heaven. It's as if it's saying where the hell has she been your whole life? Zoey's been in my face for what seems like forever and stupid me didn't know the treasure I had.

She meets my powerful thrusts with her hips and clenches her muscles around my pounding length. God, she feels so good. So fucking incredible. I pick up my pace and pound her more forcefully, coming at her fast and furious with each ragged breath. My fingertips dig so deep into her ass I'm sure my nails have marred her sweet flesh. She fists my hair, the pinching pain only adding to the intense pleasure. Sweat clusters on her forehead and chest as whimpers slip out of those kissable lips.

"Oh Brandon!" she moans yet again.

"Do. You. Like. This?" I ask, deliberately slowing down my thrusts to punctuate each word. And test her.

"Please don't stop! Harder! Faster!"

"Don't worry, baby." There's not a chance in hell I'm going to stop. My cock's been bereft for way too long. And I've dreamt about this moment forever. Going at her again at full force, I build toward climax. My cock feels like a rocket being launched into space. The main engine sequence has commenced. All revved up, I pump harder, faster. And I'm pretty sure by her impassioned sounds I'm stimulating her clit—her own little space capsule—each time I hammer her. I'm taking her to the edge, to the point of no return, and her, me. My breathing grows harsher, mixing with grunts that come from deep in my gut. I have the burning urge to kiss her delicious mouth, but so close to coming I don't want to muffle the sounds or words that spill out when she falls apart.

"Oh, oh, oh, oh," she cries out. "Brandon, I can't

hold on anymore."

"Hang in there, baby! Don't come until I tell you to."

Nodding like an automaton, she starts sobbing again. To anyone else, her desperate sounds might be construed as those of a woman mourning a loss, but to me, they're the song of a woman desperate to succumb to the one she loves.

I bang into her with reckless abandon. She holds onto me as if I'm a rollercoaster she's afraid to fall off.

"Please, Brandon. Please."

Her begging brings me to the brink. My cock's on fire. On the next bang, my cock communicates with me. *Three, two, one, we have a lift off!* I cry out, "Now, baby. Now."

On the wail of my name, her pulsing pussy combusts around my ready to explode cock. Her whole body convulses as if thrown into shock. On the next thrust, I blast into outer space, and as I pass the core of my soul to her, I cry out her name.

"ZO!!!!!!" My cock spasms for what feels like an eternity, shooting my load three times as I kiss her madly and muffle her sobs. The rest of my body goes numb while I ride out my release. I can no longer hold her up. I let go of her ass and her limp legs touch down on the ground. Still leaning against the storefront, she cradles my head in her exquisite hands. Pressing against her, I hear myself still breathing heavily as I deepen the kiss.

I don't know how long we stay in this position when I withdraw my mouth and my tongue. Her glistening eyes meet mine, the tears far from ending.

I brush them away with my thumbs. "Why are you still blubbering? What we just had was fucking amazing."

"I know," she snivels. "No one's ever made me come like that. No one. I felt like we were one."

"The same, baby. The same." And I swear that's the goddamn truth. I've never had such a mind-blowing orgasm. I left the planet with her. And a roar of her name so loud the stars heard me.

"Brandon, what are we going to do?" Her faltering voice is thick with uncertainty. Borderline despair. I can read her mind.

I cup her tear-streaked cheeks with my hands and face her squarely. "We're going to fuck our brains out, and with whatever's left, we're going to figure things out."

A glint of hope glimmers in her eyes. "My love, fuck me again."

She called me her love. This fuck has changed eve-rything. A foreboding cloud hangs over me. My chest tightens. How am I going to end it with goddamn Katrina?

Zoey's sweet rasp cuts into my anxiety. "Are you alright, Brandon?"

"Yeah." Flicking her nose, I twitch a fleeting smile. I don't tell her I was thinking about my soon-to-be ex.

Fuck Katrina. With another bruising kiss, I banish the bitch to the furthest recesses of my mind. It's time for another unforgettable fucking and I know just where I want to go. Brandon Taylor is back in control.

Chapter 21

Zoey

He's kissing me again. This time it's savage and rough. He pins my body against the stone wall while his mouth gnaws my lips and his tongue clashes with mine, thrusting and probing. The skin around my swollen lips stings beneath the brush of his stubble. The hair on the back of my neck bristles. I suck on his mouth hungrily as a tornado of swirling colors spirals from the back of my eyes, down my spine to the place I want him most. Between my thighs which are quivering with desire and dripping wet with my juices. Any worries I have are sucked into a vortex of lust. He inhabits every sense, every fiber of my being. Fuck me, Brandon! Own me! Possess me! I hitch one leg around his hips and fist him into me by the roots of his hair. I moan into his mouth when I feel his hand caress my shuddering pussy. His thumb rubs my throbbing, aching clit while he breathes into my mouth.

"Fuck, Zoey. You're still so hot, so wet for me."

"Please fuck me again, Brandon," I beg hoarsely. My desperate need for him consumes me.

Taking a small step backward, he smooths my chiffon dress and stares at me with white-hot intensity. "Baby, I'm going to take you again, but not here." With a tweak of my puckered nipples, he glances down at the cobblestones where my panties are crumpled next to my bare feet and then gives me a smug smile. "Put them back on. I don't want you to stain your pretty dress."

Mama always told me, "Baby girl, live as if there's no tomorrow." When I was a little girl, I didn't understand what that meant, but years after her senseless murder those words rang true for me.

Despite my grave insecurities about Katrina and the future, I've decided to experience Brandon Taylor to the fullest. Give him a chance. Love him as if there's no tomorrow. No risk, no gain. Even if all I end up with is pain. I banish the dark thought as I circle my arms around his taut torso on the Ducati. The poor bike isn't in great shape after Brandon crashed it in hot pursuit of me. The front fender is dented and there are dings all over the metallic violet framework. But it's still running. As we cruise down the Croisette, every little bump stimulates my vibrating clit, making me more eager to get to our destination. The hotel? I'm not sure where he's taking me when we zoom past The Carlton, but am sure when I hop off the bike there'll be a wet mark on the seat.

From crashing the Ducati, the sound system in the helmets is screwed up. I can't hear Brandon and he can't hear me. It's just as well because I want to be alone with my thoughts. It's like my head is in a bubble that's going to burst. I still can't believe this night's for real, that my remotest, wildest fantasies are a reality, but the very real throbbing between my legs tells me otherwise. Leaning into him, I can't stop re-living every minute. Brandon expressed his deep feelings toward me in heartfelt words that made me melt like a candle and gave me the most mind-blowing orgasm I ever had. Yes, I've had dozens and dozens of clitoral orgasms, most of which I've given myself, but I've never experience one from a man inside me, let alone that Big O I've read about in *Cosmopolitan* and my erotic romances. Truthfully, I thought they were some kind of urban myth, but now I know differently. They exist. Brandon Taylor set me off and sent me orbiting in space. I came and I came and I came. The euphoric waves must have lasted at least five minutes and I'm still feeling the aftermath. If I wasn't wedged against that rough stucco wall which chafed my back and kept me conscious, I would have likely fainted. Somewhere in those five minutes, my infatuation with Brandon Taylor morphed into extreme love. An intense primal need to be totally possessed by him.

Yes, I'm in love with him. Unabashedly, indisputably in love with him. While my head's in a thick cloud, a hormonal tsunami is still raging inside me. About ten minutes into our ride, he lifts my left hand off his waist and lowers it to his crotch. I feel the pulse and heat of his enormous package beneath my palm. Something about having my hand there makes me feel so calm, so connected, protected, and loved. Arousal pulses through me, revving me up like an engine. Unexpectedly, after we fly over a bump in the road, the helmets' sound system starts up again, and a soft, pitch-perfect hum fills my ears. The melody of "Unforgettable" ... it's coming from Brandon. The emotion that sweeps over me can't be put into words. Our hearts, our bodies, our minds are so powerfully connected. We're one. In every way, this incredible night and incredible man have been unforgettable. I don't let him know I can hear him except I give a little squeeze to his irresistible manhood. Closing my eyes, I sink waist-deep into blissful ecstasy.

Fifteen dreamy minutes later, we arrive at a magnificent waterfront villa located about five miles outside the center of Cannes. While the expansive palm tree-filled garden looks perfectly maintained, the windows of the imposing pink stucco mansion are boarded up.

"Who does this house belong to?" I ask Brandon as

he helps me off with my helmet.

A hint of melancholy flickers in his eyes. "A great woman who doesn't use it anymore. My mentor, Bella Stadler."

At the mention of her name, my heart skips a beat. My mind flashes back to that life-changing encounter with the beautiful woman at the Joshua Tree spa. *Lead your dreams and land them.* Her memorable words float through my head as if carried by the wings of angels. I debate whether to tell Brandon about this uncanny encounter, but his sultry voice cuts my decision-making short.

"C'mon, let's go down to the beach," he says, taking my hand.

A few minutes later after descending a steep terraced path, we're walking barefoot on a deserted, breathtaking stretch of beach along the Mediterranean. The sparkling white sand is a ribbon of moonlight against the dark sea. In the distance, I can see the lit up Palais des Festivals and the myriad yachts surrounding it.

Brandon wraps his brawny arm around my shoulders while soft, lapping waves sound in my ears. He holds me close to him.

"Don't run away from me again tonight, Zoey. I've done enough sprinting to last me a lifetime."

I laugh. "I'll try to behave."

He squeezes me. "Don't test me."

"Don't count on it." With a burst of laughter, I break away and make a mad dash toward the water.

"Screw you, Zoey. You're going to pay for this."

"Try and catch me!" I shout out, running backward.

"You're going to get it, you very naughty girl!"

I'm ready. Come and get me! On my next fired up breath, he chases after me, and in no time, he catches me. This time I don't resist and my giddy laughter fills the warm, damp air.

He cinches my waist and then flips me around so we're facing each other. Quieting, I gaze at his gorgeous face. It's lit by the moonlight—the perfect contours, his strong jaw, straight manly nose, and those beautiful eyes. The orbs are like two dark purple stars that have fallen from the sky. Then, that Satanic look that I've seen before washes over him. Every nerve in my body is on edge.

"Zoey, I want you to undress."

"Excuse me?" His words send a shockwave through me. I freeze. Somehow, despite how many fantasies I've had about him, baring myself to him has never been among them. Fear? Shame? Self-Loathing? All of the above? Yes, probably a little bit of each. Even fucking him tonight doesn't put my brain at ease. Is this my punishment for disobeying him?

"Br—"

"Do it." His voice is gruff and authoritative. But this is how he's always treated me and I've always obliged. Sweet Jesus. I'm a natural submissive. Without losing eye contact with him, I bend my arms upward and reach for the tab of the zipper. I zip it halfway down, but with my short limbs, I can't get it past the middle of my back. Brandon watches me struggle.

"Turn around," he commands, not masking his displeasure.

Silently, I do as asked. He unzips my dress, and the hiss of the parting metal teeth sends goosebumps to my skin. Gripping my shoulders, he spins me around. And then takes a few steps backward. His intimidating eyes stay glued on me.

"Take it off."

Slowly, hesitantly, I slide the chiffon dress off. Once past my hips, it glides down my legs way faster than I want it to. Before I know it, Chaz's little black number is puddled around my feet. I step out of it, my toes digging into the cool sand. I'm standing before him in just my black strapless push-up bra and a pair of skimpy lace bikinis I have no right wearing. The matching set is a part of a mysterious boxload of sexy Gloria's Secret lingerie that was messengered to my house after my visit to Chaz's studio. Neither Chaz nor Jeffrey claimed responsibility, and when I asked Brandon about it, he simply said, "No clue." I now know I shouldn't have believed him.

He holds me fierce in his gaze. I'm as still as a statue. A chill sweeps over me. His eyes travel subtly down my body and then return to my face. Now that he's seen my imperfect curvy body that's so unlike Katrina's flawless supermodel figure—and all the other "it girls" he's fucked—he won't want me anymore. Yes, he's seen me in a swimsuit once before. But this is so different. I'm so exposed. And because he's still fully clothed, I feel especially vulnerable. Maybe the night air is covering up some of my flaws. I can only hope. Mr. Taylor, I'm so not ready for my close-up.

"Zoey, stop thinking about putting the dress back on. You're beautiful in it, but you're even more beautiful without it."

I gulp so loud I can hear myself. Me beautiful? In the raw?

"Now take off your bra."

I reach my hands behind my back and undo one clasp after another. There are three of them, lined up from top to bottom. The bra falls to my feet. My full breasts quiver in the sea breeze.

"Exquisite."

I hitch a breath. Just barely.

"Now, remove those little panties."

Hooking the side strings with my thumbs, I silently slide the bikinis down my thighs. I squat to get them past my knees. Deeper and deeper with every inch until the skimpy lace concoctions are scrunched at my feet. With my hands matted to my ankles, knees bent, and my ass in the air, he tells me not to move. My eyes gaze up at him as he swaggers toward me.

He's so close to me the tip of my nose grazes his jeans. I can smell the scent of my sex on him. My senses are on high alert.

"Don't move," he repeats. "Not even a blink."

I do as I'm told. Not a blink. Not a move of a muscle. My eyes still cast upward, I watch him rip open the bottom buttons of his linen shirt. He unbuckles his leather belt, and with a whoosh, slides it out of the belt loops. He coils it around his right hand like a snake. And then uncurls it until it dangles just above his knees. He circles behind me.

A smack of fear descends on my lower back. I can see the belt between my slightly parted legs. Shit. Is he going to tie me up with it in this uncomfortable position? And fuck me without mercy? Anxiety beats in my chest like a timber drum as I await his next move.

Thwack! Before I can surmise it, the belt comes down hard on my ass. I wince. My left cheek stings like it's on fire.

"That's for running away from me. I want you to count with me."

I draw in a sharp breath. He's going to whip me again.

"Say it. One."

"One," I repeat, my voice so unsteady.

He does it. Whips me again. *Thwack!*

"Two." I groan.

And again. *Thwack!*

"Three." Tears burn my eyes.

"Do you want me to stop?"

"No!" I cry out, so turned on by the scorching pain that has my sore pussy pulsing with tremors of pleasure. Delicious warmth drips down my legs.

Thwack! Thwack! Thwack! *Thwack!* Four more times. A total of seven. All on the same spot. The incendiary sting is more than I can bear. *Mama.* My safe word is on the tip of my tongue, but I can't get my quivering lips to say it. Stifling a whimper on the next crack of the leather, I fall to my knees. Supplicating, I recall the time Pops taught me how to ride a bicycle. I was a disaster. As I was about to give up, he shared an old Japanese proverb: "Fall seven times. Stand up on eight."

"Eight," I croak, my voice jagged from my tear-infested arousal. With my trembling hands, I push myself up, back to the semi-squatting position before Brandon's next inevitable lash. His dominant voice resonates in my ear.

"Are you sorry you ran away from me, Zoey?"

Tensing my body, I prepare myself for one more pelt of his belt. *Nine.* But instead, he yanks my head back forcefully by a fistful of my hair. My eyes roll back in their sockets.

"Answer me, Zoey."

"Y-yes."

"Please show me a little respect. And I want a full sentence."

"Y-yes, sir. I-I'm sorry I ran away from you."

"Good girl. Now, promise you won't ever do it again."

"I-I promise I won't ever do it again." The words come out a little easier.

Satisfied, he releases his hand. My head falls to my thighs like a limp rag doll's while a sob pushes up from my gut.

"Fuck. Did I hurt you, Zoey?" His voice is much softer.

"N-no," I splutter through my tears.

"But you're crying. Oh, my brave little soldier. I took things too far. I just can't bear to lose you. You mean too much to me, *and* I can't help who I am. I needed to test you… to see if you could let me love you the only way I can."

"I asked for it," I whisper, lifting my head to meet his eyes. And that's the truth. I deliberately ran away from him and wanted him to punish me… until I reached tortured euphoria.

"Oh baby, you're so perfect for me. You turn my darkest desires into moonlight."

And you are my sun and my stars. On my next sniffle, a breath of cool air skims my raw ass, and then he kisses the sore spot reverently, his tongue coating it like a balm. Aah! The extreme pleasure mixes with the intense pain and creates an erotic cocktail that makes me drunk with desire. I'm addicted. I fucking want more. Yes. Please. Whip me again. Again and again and again. And then put out the fire with your love. Wishful thinking.

"Don't move your gorgeous ass, baby. Put your legs and feet together and keep your head down, pressed against your knees. Eyes closed."

I do as asked, wondering if now he's going to tie me up with the belt. At least two minutes pass. I feel his eyes on me. My nerves are on edge. Is he studying my backside? Measuring the width? Counting the dimples? Examining his handwork? Comparing me to Katrina? Having second thoughts? I wish he'd stop. My legs are beginning to shake in this yoga-like position. And my aching clit's not helping.

Finally. "Now please step out of your panties, then stand up and face me."

I can still feel his eyes on me as I slip my feet out of the leg openings and then slowly lift my torso until I'm erect again. Opening my eyes, I turn around and gasp.

Trembling, I glare at all six-foot-two of his gorgeousness. A god-like template of manly perfection alit in the glow of the full moon. I don't blink an eye.

He stares at me.

I'm bared to him. Totally bared to him.

And he's bared to me.

Chapter 22

Brandon

Fuck. In all my fantasies, I never pictured her to be so fucking beautiful. My eyes soak her in like a sponge. It takes all I have to restrain myself. It's hard. Really hard. Pun intended.

Her lips are parted, her eyes wide, the expression on her face a mixture of fear and awe. Her lustrous dark hair drapes over her shoulders like a theatrical curtain showcasing her magnificent tits. They quiver as if they're nervous about making their debut. In my head, her audience of one is applauding them. Applauding *her.* Screaming bravo. And my cock is giving her a standing ovation.

Against her chestnut hair and the navy sky, her breasts look like porcelain. Her puckered nipples like decorative, hand painted roses, the color of sweet Rosé wine. I so want to feel the weight of them in my hands and taste them. But I'm not done studying her. My eyes travel down her torso, taking in her luscious curves and full hips that seamlessly meet a pair of shapely legs. Her skin is the consistency of white velvet under the moonlight. I want to experience all of her. Every way I can.

"Come here, my beauty." I signal with my finger. She's ready for her close-up.

Hesitantly, she takes small steps toward me. Her beautiful, bountiful boobs bounce with a life of their own. My eyes stay fixed on her. My cock, already sheathed, stays on her too. Erect and at attention. In anticipation.

"You're a goddess," I tell her when she's a breath away from me. I flip her hair behind her ears so it cascades down her back. And then cup the rounded edges of her shoulders to steady her, gently massaging them to relax her. Her bones are strong, but her soft skin is like satin beneath my palms. She doesn't flinch.

"Bran—"

Lifting one hand off her shoulders, I hush her with my finger. "Shh. Just trust me. Can you do that?"

She looks up at me and nods silently, her eyes dancing with contagious lust.

I return my palm to her shoulder and then glide my hands down her smooth, silky arms and lace my fingers with hers.

"Good." I breathe into her ear and then kiss her

face. Lightly on her forehead. Her nose. Her cheeks and then her lips. Letting go of her hands, I lift mine to her lush breasts. I cup each one, savoring the fullness and weight of them. They're firm and perfectly symmetrical. I love all of her, but her cleavage is by far one of her best features. Maybe I'll fuck her tits later, but right now I just want to appreciate them. Hoisting the warm mounds in my palms, I begin squeezing and rotating them. My thumbs circle her generous nipples. The rosebud tips elongate and harden beneath my touch, turning into candy-sweet pink nuggets I yearn to suck. Squeezing her eyes shut, she arches her head back and moans.

"Am I arousing you?" I ask as I continue my ministrations.

She moans again and grips my biceps.

"Answer me, Zoey." I know her moans are my answer, but I want verification.

"Oh, Brandon. Yes."

I reward her with another kiss. This time on her neck. I suck the tender skin and then I roll my tongue up and down the length. My first real taste of her. She tastes delicious. Salty and sweet. Like salted caramel.

She moans again, this time louder and then mutters, "Oh my God," under her breath. I've obviously struck an über-sensitive spot. Her moans and groans are fucking turning me on. I so want to be inside her again, but I'm going to take it slowly. That is, if I can hold on.

My cock is throbbing, begging for re-entry. *What are you waiting for?* I hear it cry out.

My brain and cock at war, I drag my tongue down her chest until it's deep inside the well of her cleavage. I stroke it up and down, lapping up the sweat beads that have gathered on her flesh.

"Look at me, baby," I order before I move on.

She tilts her head forward and her half-mast eyes meet mine. A half-smile is all she gets from me.

I cup her right breast in both hands and lift it as my mouth goes down on it. I suck and gnaw and then circle my tongue around her aroused nipple. Pure sweetness. Her moans and groans are music to my ears. I repeat my actions with its twin. Then, I slide my hands down the sides of her taut torso, delighting in the pleasure of her luscious curves. I spend time caressing her gorgeous heart-shaped ass. She lets out a little wince and I remind myself to be gentler where she's sore. My hands brush past her womanly hips and land on her thighs. I rub them up and down, surprised by how muscular they are. Gripping them, I squat down until I'm on my knees and bury my head between her legs. Mmm. She smells of her sex and my sex, the sea, and the sky. Intoxicating.

"Spread your legs so I can sample your magnificent pussy."

With a moan, she obliges. With my hands splayed like starfish on her inner thighs, my tongue explores a new set of lips. They're just what I thought—tender and wet. And so delicious. I explore this new territory like a conqueror searching for treasure. I can feel her legs tremble and she grasps my shoulders to maintain her balance.

"Aaah!" she cries out.

I move my tongue to her clit and flick it.

"Oh my God!"

I flick it again and again and again. Faster and faster. My aerobic tongue moving in all directions. The responsive nub hardens and swells. So engorged and gorgeous. Her nails dig into me. Her breathing grows shallow and desperate whimpers fill my ears.

"You're making me come again," she pants out. "Oh, please... Brandon."

That's the plan, baby, I say silently, not wanting to break contact with her. She has my permission. With just one suck of her clit, she explodes.

I feel like Moses when he discovered the Promised Land.

Chapter 23

Zoey

I haven't recovered from the last two major orgasms and I'm about to have another. I'm not quite sure how I got into this position. Maybe I just fainted. I'm lying on the sand, my head and back on Brandon's linen shirt. My splayed legs are hooked over his shoulders and he's hovering over me. His hands are anchored in the sand on either side of my face.

His enormous cock is buried deep inside me, pounding me ruthlessly. I swear he's going to make my pussy black and blue. I clench him with my inner muscles, bucking into him with my hips and meeting every forceful thrust.

"Holy Jesus. You're so fucking tight and wet," he breathes out. "I can't get enough of you."

And I can't get enough of him. So consumed by the moment, I can't get the words out. He's insatiable. And so am I.

His strokes are long, powerful, and purposeful. With each one, his rock-hard cock rubs my clit, stimulating it and hitting that magic spot inside me I never knew I had. My breathing is labored, my skin heated; my heart racing. Everything's condensed in a haze of lust and love.

"I want to own your body, Zoey."

"I'm yours," I pant out.

"I so needed to hear that. You're so fucking beautiful."

He called me beautiful again. The word makes me unravel as I moan with tortured ecstasy.

"Tell me what you want, baby."

There are so many things I want. I want this night to never end. I want him to never leave me. I want his mouth on mine… all over me. I want, I want, I want… Fuck. I can't think straight anymore.

"Do you want to come?"

Oh God, yes. The Mediterranean may be calm, but a tidal wave of epic proportions is sweeping through me, taking every cell in its midst.

"Zoey, I need words."

"Yes! Please make me come."

"Baby, don't hold back. I want you to fall apart into a million pieces so I can put you back together and then make you fall apart again."

"Oh, Brandon!" My body convulses and a sea of

love meets his own volcanic eruption head on. He roars out my name yet again and collapses on top of me, taking my legs with him. For the first time, I feel his nakedness all over mine. Blanketing me with his warmth. I've never felt so comfortable—or beautiful— in my own skin.

After collapsing on me and staying there for a while, Brandon rolls over and repositions us so that we're both on our backs. My head is on his chest. One of his arms cradles me while the hand of the other draws lazy circles around my nipples and then my navel. It's ticklish and delicious. We both gaze up at the starry sky while the Mediterranean softly serenades us. It's as if no one else exists except the two of us.

"How do you feel?" he asks, breaking the silence.

"Fucked."

"In a good way or bad way?"

"In the best way. But I'm sore. Very sore."

"Where?"

"All over." And that's the truth. My back smarts from grinding against the rough stucco, my ass throbs from the belting, my legs ache from running away from him and from being stretched, and my face stings from the coarseness of his stubble. But where I feel it the most is between my inner thighs. My pussy's on fire.

"Show me where it hurts the most."

I take his hand and put it on my pussy. He caresses it, the rawness giving way to arousal against the gentle friction of his fingertips.

"I gave it to you good, huh?" His voice is laced with smug victory. "Was it too hard for you?"

"I don't think I can walk." *I loved every fucking minute.*

"Do you think you'll be able to walk down the red carpet with me tomorrow night?"

Of course, I will and can't wait, but the actress in me says: "Not sure."

On my next heartbeat, he stands and scoops me up in his strong, loving arms.

"What are you doing?"

He shoots me a cocky smile. "I'm going to heal you. I can't afford to have you out of commission tomorrow night...or tonight for that matter."

Two minutes later, to my utter shock, we're deep in the Mediterranean. He's still holding me, but now I'm facing him, my arms and legs wrapped tightly around him. The water is surprisingly warm and while the saltiness initially stung my soreness, now it's soothing. I cling to him like a life preserver, and while I know this is a gentle sea, my fear of the ocean has crept back into me.

"How do you feel?" he breathes in my ear between delicious kisses.

"Better. But I'm anxious." Truthfully, I don't know what I'm afraid of. There are no waves and the current isn't strong. And he's holding me.

"Are there sharks?"

"Yup."

I gasp.

He smiles smugly. "Just one … me. I want to eat you up alive, my sexy little beast."

Before I can punch him, he latches his lips on to mine, consuming me with another tongue-driven, passionate kiss. He cups the back of my head while I fist his hair, deepening and prolonging it. As our tongues glide together in some kind of synchronized swim, waves of bliss roll through me. I don't want to let him go. My fear of the ocean is abruptly replaced by my fear of losing him. And the reality is he's not mine to be lost. He belongs to another. Katrina. For the first time since leaving the restaurant, her name sears my mind, my heart, and my soul. Why didn't he break up with her before this trip? He hasn't told me and I'm too afraid to ask him. Apprehension ripping through me, I pull away.

"Brandon, fuck me!" A desperate plea. A defense mechanism? I'm suddenly treading water in a sea of doubt.

He smooths my unruly damp hair. "No, baby. As much I'd like to, and believe me, I'm hard as nails, I need you whole tomorrow. You've had enough of me tonight."

I *can't* get enough of him. I want him in the worst way. With all my heart. Tears, as salty as the sea, fill my eyes. I blink them back.

"Please." Mama's magic word.

"Baby, what's the matter? Why do you look like you're about to cry again? Seriously, I'm not good with tears I can't control. They drive me crazy."

"Good crazy?"

"No, bad crazy with you." His violet eyes, dark with night, pierce mine.

"What do you mean?"

"Because I care about you." He traces my lips with a finger. "And have this all-consuming need to protect you. So, when you cry tears I don't understand that have nothing to do with me fucking you hard, I think I'm failing."

His words eat away at me. I'm fraught with emotion. *He cares about me.* This is not the first time he's said that, and I flashback to the time he told me this while I was convalescing from my concussion. Somehow, those words directed at me tonight strike an especially deep chord. A traitor tear escapes.

He kisses it away. "Zoey, please don't do this to me. Stop crying. And that's an order."

"Okay," I whisper.

A grateful sexy smile lights up his face. "C'mon, let's go for a swim before we head back. There's nothing like swimming in the sea at night. I'll stay close to you."

Knowing he'll be there for me, all my inhibitions and fears melt away. A renewed sense of security and strength washes over me. On my next breath, I'm under the water with Brandon by my side. Other than the shadow of his chiseled body and the bubbles we make, all I see is blackness. The blackness envelops me and is magical, instilling me with peacefulness and a passion for survival. Making me brave the precarious unknown that awaits me. *Lead your dreams and land them . . .* then live them. Right now, Brandon Taylor is mine and I'm his. The swim is sublime. And so is his kiss under the water.

I love you, I love you, I love you, I say to myself silently. For as long as my breath allows. I may be swimming in the sea, but I'm drowning in love.

Chapter 24

Zoey

Brandon insists on me wearing his linen shirt over my dress after our swim to keep warm as well as on carrying me back to the Ducati. And when we get to The Carlton after leaving the banged up bike and our helmets with the valet, he insists on carrying me through the lobby to the elevator. Not only doesn't he want me to walk because of my fragile condition, I'm shoeless. I tossed my heels into a trash can in The Old City when I ran away from him. Barefoot, I could step on something nasty and get hurt. He's so overprotective, but I give in to him. And besides, it's fun. I'm riding him piggyback-style—something I used to love doing with Pops when I was a little girl. I haven't done it in years.

"Hold on," he says as he bounces me toward the elevator.

"I am." I start giggling at the double meaning of my words. My legs are wrapped around him, his arms hooked under my knees, and my arms draped over his broad shoulders. The ride is stimulating my nipples, the friction of his bare skin against them arousing me. I swear there must be a power cord that plugs into my pussy. And it's sparking. I could easily come again.

The Carlton is buzzing. International movers and shakers occupy the bar, already making strategic partnerships and distribution deals for the year ahead. I spot Blake Burns in an animated conversation with two Japanese broadcasters. I hope he doesn't see me. And then again, I don't care. Thanks to tight security, paparazzi are nowhere in sight.

When we get to the elevator, Brandon punches the UP button. To my relief, a car comes quickly and the doors part instantly. Mortification races through me. Standing before us is Blake Burns's lovely wife, Jennifer, wearing a sexy red cocktail dress I recognize from Chaz's collection. Gah! What is she going to think? Brandon's bare-chested; I'm wearing his shirt and have a tangle of wet hair, and we're both sprinkled with a fine layer of sand. I smile sheepishly and squeak, "Hi."

She steps out of the car and the doors close behind her before we can get in.

She gives us the once over and then flashes a big smile. "Looks like you guys had fun."

"We went for a swim," Brandon says without reservation.

And that's not all we did. It's hard to tell if Jennifer knows we fucked our brains out. No fan of Katrina's, she's not passing judgment.

"After you wash up, why don't you both join Blake and me for drinks?"

Unwavering, Brandon replies, "Thanks, but we're going to pass with MIP starting tomorrow and the big *Kurt Kussler* event in the evening. Plus, I have some work to do with Zoey."

"Totally understand. Don't work her *too* hard." Jennifer winks at him. Oh yeah, she so knows. "I'll see you both tomorrow at The Palais. Enjoy the rest of your evening."

"You too," says Brandon before she heads toward the bar area. He slaps the UP button again and the elevator doors immediately re-open. With me still riding his back, we step inside the elegantly appointed lift.

"Do you think she suspects something?" I ask Brandon as the doors close.

"Frankly, my dear, I don't give a damn."

Drunk with love, I burst into laughter. "That's so not original."

"Shut. Up. Or I'll have to fuck your mouth into silence."

Not knowing if I'm going to laugh my head off or

suck him off, I reach for my floor button. But Brandon grabs my wrist and stops me midway.

"What do you think you're doing?" I ask as he forces my hand down.

He answers my question with a question. "Where do you think you're going?"

"To my room."

"Nothing doing. You're sleeping with me."

My breath hitches. I kiss him everywhere I can as he waves his key card over the button marked PH—the exclusive penthouse floor. The elevator smoothly ascends with no stops. I can't stop loving him.

Brandon's Sean Connery suite is almost as big as his house. It's got to be close to five thousand square feet. Stunning black and white photos of the debonair actor in his James Bond finery line the walls and meet my eyes first. The rest of the décor is classical, the rooms tastefully filled with plush furnishings in muted tones of brown, beige, and tan. Complementary textured rugs cover the dark hardwood floors while creamy silk curtains accent the floor-to-ceiling windows overlooking a terrace and the city. The panoramic view of the Croisette and the Mediterranean is breathtaking.

Brandon takes me directly to the ginormous bathroom. What makes it really spectacular is that it's circular—the sexy, curvy shape dictated by its position directly beneath one of the hotel's Belle Époque arched domes. All creamy marble and shiny chrome with pale blue accents, it's a suite within a suite, with separate bathing and toilet areas. The lights are dim. He sets me down on a marble vanity and then reaches for the wall phone. He holds the receiver to his ear and speaks into it. My eyes fix on his flexed bicep and the rigid muscles of his sculpted back. His skin is bronzed velvet. Christ, he's gorgeous. A fucking sex god. Even his sultry voice excites me.

"*Oui,* this is Monsieur Taylor in the Sean Connery suite. I'd like to order two hot chocolates, two shots of crème de cacao, and a plate of praline truffles if you don't have M&Ms." He pauses and then smiles. "*Oui, beaucoup de* whipped cream."

He hangs up the phone and faces me. "Are you okay with that? I thought maybe we'd get hungry later."

"*Oui*, Monsieur Taylor." I put on my best French accent and make my voice as breathy as possible. Truthfully, the only thing I'm hungering for is his cock.

A saucy smile tugs at his lips. "I like it when you call me that. It turns me on. I want you to call me 'monsieur' for the rest of the evening. Deal?"

"*Oui*, monsieur." My sexy, throaty voice is deeper and breathier. I'm channeling Simone Signoret. "What's our next activity?"

He eyes me sheepishly. "I want to watch you use the bidet."

"Excuse me?"

"The bidet." He lifts me off the vanity and leads me to a white porcelain basin that's right next to the toilet. About the same height, it resembles an oblong sink with a pair of faucets.

"What's this for?" I ask suspiciously.

"It's going to clean the sand out of your ass *and* make your pussy feel better."

"My pussy's just fine," I lie. It's still sore as hell, but I don't want him to think I'm unfuckable. Then again, maybe that's what he has in mind. Restoration. Then fucking me senseless again until I cry. My heart skips a beat with another thought. Or maybe fucking me hard in the butt?

He flicks my nose. "Trust me."

"Aren't you going to turn the water on?"

"Sit," he orders with a playful slap on my sore ass ... that turns *me* on.

My skin prickles. I do as I'm told. I plop down on the edge of the basin, scrunching up my chiffon dress and pulling my panties down to my knees. Much the same as I would do if I were taking a pee. The rim of the porcelain basin is a cool contrast to my heated ass.

Brandon rolls his eyes at me. "Baby, it's not a toilet. You need to take off your panties and straddle it."

"Oh." I feel totally stupid, but the amused smile on his face saves me from humiliation.

I slide off my panties. The cotton crotch is soaked and laced with a few granules of sand. Brandon snatches them from me while I reposition myself. My legs are spread-eagled over the basin. My exposed pussy is in full view. Brandon examines it.

"Fuck. Your pussy's really red. And swollen."

I glance down. Gah! It is.

Not wasting a second, Brandon turns the water on full force.

"Aah!" I squeal. The basin doesn't begin to fill. Instead, to my utter surprise and delight, powerful jets of warm water shoot upward, hitting my inflamed genitals.

I sigh loudly again. It feels amazing. Yes, the water is soothing, but it's also stimulating my über-sensitive clit and sending jets of pleasure through my core.

Brandon breaks into a wide smile. "That feels good, *n'est-ce pas?*"

"*Oui, oui*, monsieur." Holy cow! I'm totally getting off on it. I rock my hips to maximize the delicious sensation. My breathing grows erratic and little oohs and aahs clog my throat. Brandon's eyes stay on me, his voyeuristic expression one of a man totally entertained.

"Jesus, Zoey. You're fucking unbelievable."

I flash a little smile at what I think is a compliment. My arousal is consuming me.

"My beauty, I'm going to watch you make yourself come. Hands behind your head."

"I can't use my fingers?"

He smirks. "Trust me, you won't have to. Now, do

it before I tie up those talented hands of yours." With a wicked glint, he twists my skimpy panties into a rope. Holy shit! The kinky bastard definitely means business.

I do as I'm told, the sweet sensation of an orgasm already on the brink. The pressure's building fast and furiously. My head rolls around like a rag doll's as I get closer to the edge. The hem of my layered dress is getting soaked by the spray as is Brandon's linen shirt, but I don't give a damn. The relentless pressure between my legs mounts and my breathing grows more ragged, the moans and groans more vocal. More desperate until I can't take it anymore and I'm crying, "Oh my God," over and over. All hell breaks loose, and as waves of ecstasy crash through me, I sob out my orgasm. I think I've lost consciousness. My head hangs loosely between my legs with my arms limply beside them.

"Bravo!" A single word brings me back to the land of the living. I look up. Brandon's hovering over me, grinning broadly.

"That was the most beautiful performance I've ever seen."

I suppose I should get up and curtsey, but I don't have the strength to stand. And even if I could, my legs would likely buckle. I don't even have it in me to say thank you. Breathless, I simply twitch a small smile.

Brandon brushes back my hair, still damp from our swim, and then bends down to kiss my scalp. "How does your pussy feel?"

I still can't get my brain to communicate with my mouth.

"Answer me, Zoey." That bossy voice again!

"Um, uh, excellent," I finally manage. It really does feel less sore, but it's still throbbing from my latest outrageous orgasm.

"Let me see." Brandon takes a few steps back and casts his eyes on my cleft. A small but fiendish smile plays on his lips. "Much better. It's still a little red but not as swollen. I'm tempted to take you right over the bidet."

From behind? I gulp. I thought he wasn't going to fuck me again. Every nerve ending buzzes. I can't tell if it's fear or excitement that's making my heart pound. Climaxing from the bidet was mind-blowing, but climaxing with him is like falling off the edge of a cliff.

Brandon tugs at his lower lip with his thumb ... that insanely sexy thing he does when he's deep in thought. I wonder—what is he thinking?

"On second thought, sit. Relax. I'm going to draw us a bath."

Catching my breath, I watch as he leaves me and rounds a blue mosaic partition. I notice for the first time he's missing his belt. Guess he must have left it behind at the beach. I bet I'll miss it more than he does. I close my eyes. The intense memory of that erotic experience unwinds in my head like a scene from a surreal movie, my still fiery ass a vivid reminder. Oh God, it hurt! As I relive it, every nerve ending along my flesh sparks as if there's a live electrical wire running through the connective tissue of my body, especially the super-charged bundle of nerves between my legs. I hiss. To say I didn't love it would be a lie. In my massage classes, I learned that pain can equal pleasure. What I experienced with Brandon was exquisite pleasure. There's pain in love. And love in pain.

Brandon disappears from sight, but from where I sit, I can hear him turn on the water. It pours out full blast. While the water continues to gush, he returns to me. At the sound and scent of him, I snap open my eyes. He helps me off the bidet. Coming from that spread-legged position and my trance-like state, I'm hardly what you'd call graceful getting to my feet. He holds me steady, his hands on my waist. I fix my dress, remembering I'm pantiless, and then tug at his belt loops.

"You know, you left your belt at the beach."

He glances down and then winks at me. "Don't worry. I have plenty of them. Behave."

Drawing me in tighter, he nuzzles that hypersensitive part of my neck. I squirm with pleasure. It sends a rush of tingles to my already over-sensitized sex. The throbbing won't calm down.

"You sure you're okay?"

"Yeah."

"How does your pussy feel now?"

"Fuckable."

He chortles. "You're a natural stand-up comic."

"That's not funny."

"C'mon. The bath is probably ready."

Piece by piece, he undresses me, beginning with his shirt. He then unzips the dress and lifts it over my head. After tossing both garments to the marble floor on top of my panties, he unhooks my bra, and once again, I'm totally naked. Bared to him. With lust dancing in his eyes, he reverently kisses each of my breasts. And then twists the nipples, just enough to inflict the perfect measure of pain. I let out a light gasp.

He squeezes the buds harder between his fingers. "Jesus. You so fucking turn me on."

"Does that mean we're going to fuck again?" I breathe out, my arousal taunting me. I search his hooded eyes for the promise of more.

"Maybe. But you're not going to know until you take off my jeans."

That's all that separates me from his cock. The strain of his erection against his fly is so palpable I can practically hear it crying out to be set free. A pool of wet heat gathers between my inner thighs. I'm still so fucking sore, but I want him again in the worst way. While he continues to tweak my sensitive, hardening nipples, I hastily unbutton his jeans, unzip the fly, and shove them down his taut legs. His gigantic cock as I imagined is ready for action. While the tub continues to fill, he kicks off his shoes, steps out of his jeans, and then draws me close to him.

"I so fucking want you, Zoey." He rubs his dick against my slick pussy before smacking a hot kiss on my forehead. "C'mon let's get into the bath before I bury my cock inside you and have you overflowing with my cum."

He lifts me into his arms and carries me to the tub. My eyes practically pop out of my sockets. Holy cow! I've never seen a tub like this before. Circular, massive, and at least four-feet deep, it dominates the expansive space. He sets me down gently and turns off the water. The tub is almost filled to the brim, and a thick layer of bubbly white foam coats the water's surface. The intoxicating scent of lavender drifts to my nose. His words replay in my head. *I so fucking want you, Zoey.* Again! I'm delirious with desire. This fairy tale better never end.

Brandon steps into the tub first, one long muscular leg after the other. He gracefully lowers himself to a sitting position, until his body all but disappears beneath the foamy bubbles. Leaning back against the basin, he lets out a loud contented "Aah." I wonder—is that the sexy sound he makes when he gets a blowjob?

"Get your sweet ass in here," he orders, curtailing my ruminations.

I carefully get into the enormous round tub. Brandon grips my hand while I lower myself and sink my hips between his steepled legs. He slides me tight against him so we're flesh to flesh. His thighs press against me and I can feel his hard length along my backside. The bubbles come up almost to my chin, covering all of me including my breasts. I feel awkward.

"Brandon, I've never taken a bath with a man." *Let alone, a man like you,* I add silently. The truth, with my fear of drowning, I never took baths. Not until Brandon taught me how to swim did I indulge in one and since then, very few.

"So this is a first?"

"Yes," I say timidly. Everything on this dreamy trip has been a first with him, with the earth-shattering orgasms he's given me topping the list.

Drawing me closer to him, he nuzzles the back of my neck. "Then, I'm going to have to make it unforgettable."

Another yes! This one silent but punctuated with an exclamation point. My head folds forward. I'm so ready for him.

With one hand, he grabs a large sponge, and then with the other, he lifts up my long wet hair. He begins to run circles along my upper back and shoulders, and as gentle as they are, I flinch.

"What's the matter baby? Am I hurting you?"

"No, no, I'm okay."

He sponges me again, and again, despite his light

touch, I can't help jerking.

I hear him splash aside the bubble-coated water.

"Shit. Did I do this?"

He must have discovered all the scratches on my back from the wall-banger fuck. The stucco scraped my skin and bruised my spine. It's not really his fault.

"No," I reply softly. "If walls could talk…"

"Oh, baby." He instantly flutter kisses all the blemishes. So tenderly, it's as if butterflies are dancing across my back. I hum.

And then, I yelp, "Ow!" His teeth have come down on me. He's bitten my right shoulder. Before I can ask for an explanation, he sucks the wound. Pain mixes with pleasure, arousing me.

"That's going to be a souvenir of this bath," he whispers in my ear. "I want you to always remember it."

Believe me. "I will," I murmur as he kisses me again.

"Are you on birth control?" he breathes against the nape of my neck between little nips and gnaws.

"Yes."

"Good. I want to fuck you again. Can you—"

"Handle it?"

"That's not what I was going to ask you. You don't have much choice in that department. I make those decisions."

The control he exerts over me turns me on. A surge

of desire hurtles through me. Apologizing, I ask him what he was going to say.

"Zoey, can you *trust* me?"

He's used that word a lot tonight. And I've fallen for it each time. Suddenly, it's an ambiguous word I distrust; it frightens me. The image of Katrina comes back to haunt me like a specter. Despite the hot bath, a shiver slithers down my spine. "What do you mean?" I ask, my voice shaky.

"I'm not wearing a condom."

Oddly, a condom was the last thing on my mind. Reservation plays an unexpected game of tug of war with want. He's probably been with hundreds of women ...

"I know what you're thinking. I'm clean. When I was in the hospital, they tested me for everything."

"But you've been with Katrina." Just breathing in the bitch could result in a sexually transmitted disease.

"I haven't fucked her since my release."

"But you said sex with her sucked."

"That's not what I meant. Semantics. It's been non-existent." He pauses. "Please, baby, let's stop talking about her. She's six thousand miles away. I'll deal with her when we get back to LA. For all intents and purposes, she doesn't exist."

She *does* exist. It still disturbs me that he didn't break up with before our trip. There must be some reason, but I can't ask him. I know him too well. He may be hung like a horse, but he's as stubborn as a mule. End of discussion.

I force Katrina to the back of my mind as he smothers my back with more kisses and puts a hand between my legs. The caress of my aching clit magically makes her disappear into thin air. In my mind, I hear my pussy crying out for him. *He's* all that exists.

"So, baby, are you cool with me fucking you unprotected?"

He applies more pressure. I throw my head back and moan. My answer. Sweet surrender.

"Sit on me, baby."

Gripping my hips, he shifts me a little and then lifts me up several inches. I feel the tip of his dick at my entrance. Just as I begin to lower myself on his magnificent length, the doorbell sounds through the intercom.

"Fuck," grumbles Brandon. "That must be room service."

I silently curse. Of all times to come! Lifting me off him, my beautiful lover stands, making a splash, and then steps out of the tub. My eyes stay glued on his gorgeous body dripping wet with sudsy water and his enormous erection, committing every slick contour to memory, while he wraps an oversized fluffy white towel around his hips. It's low enough to showcase his washboard abs and his perfect pelvic V. He's just so fucking sexy. Pure manly perfection. Seriously, he'll be

People Magazine's "Sexiest Man Alive" even when he's dead.

"Don't move. I'll be right back." He shoots me a cocky smile. "We'll pick up right where we left off."

"I'll be waiting, Prince Charming." *Hurry!*

"Aren't you missing a word?"

I quirk a knowing smile. "Monsieur Prince Charming."

Satisfied, he blows me an air kiss with those kissable lips and dashes out of the bathroom. Humming "Unforgettable," I relax in the tub, stretching out my legs and leaning my head against the backboard. I close my eyes and let glorious memories of the last twenty-four hours dance in my head to make up for my emptiness.

Five minutes pass, and my sweet memories are interrupted by angry voices coming from another room. My eyes flutter open. Is Brandon having some kind of argument with the hotel help? Maybe they forgot something? Knowing Brandon as well as I do, that would piss him off.

"Why the hell didn't you let me know?" I hear Brandon yell.

The hotel kitchen ran out of whipped cream? Concerned and curious, I get out of the steep tub and grab one of the plush terry cloth robes hanging from a hook within arm's reach. Without towel drying myself, I shrug it on and loosely belt it. It feels yummy.

"Brandon, is everything okay?" I ask upon entering the spacious living room.

And then I shudder to a halt and my jaw crashes to the floor. All air leaves my lungs.

Standing at the doorway is Katrina, dressed to the nines and clutching Gucci. Her cat-green eyes clash with mine as she reddens with fury.

"Brandon, what the hell is she doing here?" she shrieks as Gucci jumps out of her arms and runs over to me. He laps my bare toes with sweet kisses, but I'm too paralyzed with shock to acknowledge the affectionate little dog.

"We need to talk." Brandon's tone is sharp.

"We sure as hell do." Her venomous eyes clash with mine yet again. They fire poisonous darts in my direction, each one piercing a piece of me.

"Get the fuck out of here, you fat cunt!"

My chest tightens painfully. If Brandon used that filthy word, it would make me feel sexy and beautiful. She's made me feel vilified. Ashamed of myself. Like nothing more than a lowlife whore.

Tears sting the back of my eyes. I fight them back. I'm not going to let her see me cry. No fucking way.

My eyes lock with Brandon's. His expression goes from rage to compassion with a dash of lust and remorse. I face him squarely.

"Brandon, it's best I leave," I say in my calmest, most dignified voice. Inside I'm falling apart.

"Zoey—" He jogs over to me and puts his hands on my shoulders.

"Please." My voice is a desperate plea. He releases me.

I march toward the door with my head held high. Truthfully, I'm a shuddering, spineless mound of goo. My bones are so liquid that only pure pride and willpower hold me up.

"Zoey, don't go," Brandon pleads.

Harnessing all the strength I have, I continue toward the door and say nothing because anything I say will be all wrong. And even worse, if I open my mouth, the tears may start falling. Stepping aside, Katrina keeps her evil eye on me. I look away and don't look back.

I hear Brandon curse under his breath. "Baby, I'll text you later."

I barely hear the last word. The door to his suite slams behind me, and the dam holding back my tears bursts open. Waterworks flood my eyes. My walk a stagger, I make my way to the elevator, my heart more shattered than my battered body.

Chapter 25

Brandon

"What the fuck is wrong with you?"

"Fuck you, Brandon!"

An unexpected, devastating hurricane with winds gusting at a hundred miles an hour storms through my hotel suite.

Hurricane Katrina. Actually, Katrina is more of a tornado, a whirling dervish of hate, rage, and madness. There's no calming her down. Rationality has no meaning with this insane force of nature. All I can do is stay out of the path of her wrath, and that's virtually impossible. I should have fled the room with smart little Gucci, but I'm on major damage control.

"Goddamn it, Katrina. Stop it!"

There is no stopping her. She destroys everything in her wake, including the room service delivery, which showed up shortly after her arrival. I watch as she knocks over the tray table, sending everything crashing to the floor. The shot glasses shatter while the hot chocolate spreads like sludge on the cream-colored rug. After stomping on the truffles, she attacks the bar, hurling one bottle of alcohol at me after another. Within minutes, my suite is strewn with broken plates, lamps, bottles, and vases. Even framed artwork has been recklessly tossed to the floor. Thousands of dollars worth of damage. I'm going to have a lot of explaining to do to the hotel management, but right now that's the least of my problems.

"Why the hell didn't you tell me you were coming?" I sputter, ducking a tumbler. She misses and it shatters against a wall. Thank God, Blake Burns and his wife, who are occupying the Grace Kelly suite next door, are downstairs and can't hear what's going on. Blake warned me my fiancée was capable of a lot of shit. But this? Katrina's gone completely mental.

"I tried to call you, you prick, but you didn't pick up."

"I had my phone turned off," I lie, clearly remembering her invasive call during my dinner with Zoey. "I thought you were visiting your father for a couple of days…shooting a segment of your series." I don't tell her that I tried to call her before I left for MIP because at this point it's futile. Even if I'd broken up with her before the trip, there's no doubt in my mind the psycho bitch would have caught the first plane here—even chartered one with my card if she had to.

"My plans changed." With a grunt, she hurls a portrait of Sean Connery at me. It narrowly misses and crashes to the floor. "The penitentiary wouldn't let my crew inside, so we turned around after I said hello to Daddy."

She hurls another photo.

"For fuck's sake, stop it, Katrina!" I yell at her.

"You fucking son of a bitch. How the hell could you sleep with that slut?"

Her toxic insult makes my blood curdle. I feel my face reddening with rage. "Zoey is not a slut."

"She's a fucking fat pig. I'm surprised you could even find your way into her."

"Put a lid on it, Katrina!" I bark, incensing her further. I draw sharp breaths in and out of my nose and clench my fists by my sides as my mad fiancée rages through the room in search of more things she can hurl at me. Yes, I need to restrain her, but I'm afraid I'll do something far worse. Like assault her. Shit! That's the last thing I need before the premiere of the *Kurt Kussler* season finale tomorrow night. Make that the next to last thing. I need Katrina here like another hole in my head.

Uncontrollable, she flings an ashtray at me, and this time it smacks me in the ribs. My chest smarts. Keeled over with pain, I think about calling security, but that could open a Pandora's box too. Reduced to throwing harmless pillows at me, she continues on her ruthless rampage.

"Oh, and did the little whore suck your dick? I bet with her appetite she had no problem swallowing."

"SHUT UP, Katrina!"

She comes to a sudden halt and spins around to face me. Her manic eyes laser into me, but they fail to unnerve me.

"Katrina, what I did is wrong. But I have no regrets because it felt right. I think we need to separate and find out if whatever we had before my accident can be restored."

"What exactly are you saying?"

"We should see other people."

Her face screws up so tightly it must hurt. "Are you out of your fucking mind? We're getting married in three weeks. The whole world will be watching."

"I think we should call off the wedding."

"You *are* out of your fucking mind."

Maybe I am. But one thing I'm clear about is my connection with Zoey. My adorable, fuckable, big-hearted assistant. She's everything I want in a woman. Feisty but compliant. She's always been there for me. At my beck and call. The perfect submissive for my dominant ways. She takes the pain I inflict on her with grace and fortitude and savors the pleasure I give her with pure unadulterated inhibition. I'm in awe of her. Come on. Who am I kidding? I'm in love. Totally, unabashedly in love. I mentally kick myself. Dammit. I should have just broken up with Katrina for good. A clean break with no hope for a future. Maybe it's not too late.

"Katrina—"

"*You* shut the fuck up." Her eyes narrow. "And listen to me."

"I'll give you any—"

"Brandon, what part of listen don't you get? There's no way out of this wedding. You call it off, and I will make your life a living hell. Beginning tonight."

My eyes stay on her as she bends down and picks up a fragment from a vase. I gasp in shock as she drags the sharp, jagged edge along the inside of her arm. Blood pours from the nine-inch gash.

"Jesus, Katrina, what the fuck are you doing?"

She smirks at me. "It's not what I'm doing. It's what *you're* doing. Should I call security and tell them we had a fight and you tried to kill me?"

"Katrina, you're fucking sick."

She snickers. "Wrong, darling. I'm fucking smart. Watch and learn."

To my horror, she picks up the phone that's on an end table by the couch and then taunts me by circling her index finger around the keypad. "I'm calling security."

"Katrina. Put. The. Phone. Down."

"No. Not until you swear you're going to marry me." She taps the keypad with a long crimson fingernail. "Well?"

Tap. Tap. Tap. Tap. Tap. The tapping gets faster, louder. Drowning out my rapid heartbeat.

The psycho bitch purses her glossed lips. "Hmm. I think I'll just dial '0' for the front desk."

Tap. Tap. Tap. Tap. Tap.

"Oh, I'm sure you know ... makeup works wonders. While I'm waiting—those French frogs are so slow!—I'll apply a little eye shadow. A few black and blues. A black eye will especially look good."

Jesus. She's sick. So, so sick.

It gets worse. She rubs her bleeding arm across her face.

"Nothing like being punched and getting a bloody nose."

And then, she rakes a hand through her perfectly coiffed hair and starts yanking out handfuls.

"Gotta make it look like a struggle, *n'est-ce pas?*" she purrs, tossing the platinum clumps to the floor. "Don't worry, darling. It'll grow back by the wedding. Or I'll just get a few weaves."

She smirks. "After I take a few selfies and photos, I'm going to speed dial TMZ and give them an exclusive scoop—'Brandon Taylor beat me, mutilated me, and sexually abused me.' In a heartbeat, it'll be all over the Internet and the cover story of every major tabloid."

Bile rises to my throat and I swallow it back. "I'll

contest everything."

She scoffs at me. "Oh, Brandy-Poo, who do you think they're going to believe? America's beautiful, supermodel-thin 'It Girl'? Or America's gun-wielding, strapping action hero?"

Oh, God! She's right! Panic grips me by the balls. There's no stopping her insanity. A media maelstrom is in the making at the worst possible time.

Tap. Tap. Tap. "Time's up, Brandon."

Shit. "I swear, I swear." I vomit the words in a frenzy.

"You swear what?"

"I swear I'll marry you."

She shoots me a wicked, triumphant smile. "Good. But I want you to do one other thing."

"Anything."

"I want you to fire the fat-ass bitch."

Christ. What have I gotten myself into? I say I will without meaning it. "Now, Katrina, give me the phone."

"Here." She hurls it at me. I catch it just before it hits me in the eye.

She bends down and retrieves a linen napkin from the floor. She wraps it around her still bleeding wound. "*I* will be attending tomorrow night's premiere with you. Understood?"

I nod.

"And if I see that fat whore anywhere in sight, you can be sure the press and paparazzi will see the damage you caused." She rubs her bandaged arm. "For all intents and purposes, we should look like the happiest, most in love couple in the world...Bratrina."

Fucking Bratrina. I'm an actor. I'm going to have to act the part. The psycho bitch has got me between a rock and a hard place. What a fucking nightmare! I blow out a whoosh of air to release tension.

"Katrina, we should sleep in separate hotel rooms tonight. To cool off."

"Be my guest," she says smugly.

I dial the front desk and ask for another room, not saying for whom. Nothing's available; the hotel's sold out. With MIP, probably every hotel in Cannes is. I should throw her out onto the street on her bony ass, but that comes with its own share of serious repercussions. Fuck. I'm stuck here with her.

"Katrina, why don't you take the master suite?" While there are four sweeping bedrooms in my deluxe accommodations, offering her less than the best can so easily turn against me. "I'm going to clean up this mess and hang out here for a while."

She grabs her monstrous designer bag, which she left by the door, and pulls out her cell phone. *Click. Click. Click.* Dammit. She's taking photos of both her bloody, bandaged arm and the wreckage. And then she makes some pained faces complete with crocodile tears and takes a few selfies. Nausea washes over me. Evidence.

"Just in case." She slips her phone back into her purse and fakes a yawn. "I do need my beauty sleep, especially in light of the big event tomorrow. And I think with a little space between us, you'll come to your senses."

She saunters toward my bedroom. "The porter will be up shortly with all my luggage. And a bottle of Cristal. Just have him bring everything directly to my room."

"Fine." I stab the word at her.

"And, darling, don't forget to do what I asked you to do. I *never* want to see that fat cunt again!"

She disappears and I begin to clean up the remains of her rampage. It takes me over an hour. Emotionally and physically drained, I sink into the couch where The Gooch, who's come out of hiding, shortly joins me. A small comfort.

I weakly pet him and look to him for answers. He cocks his head and stares at me with his big brown puppy eyes.

It's hopeless. With the little dog curled up beside me, I bury my face in my hands.

Zoey, Zoey, Zoey.

What the fuck am I going to do?

Chapter 26

Zoey

I'm curled up in an easy chair in complete darkness, the blackout curtains drawn. The only light in the room comes from my cell phone, which is on my lap. I glance down at it. It's one a.m. It's been over two hours. My stomach is twisted in a torturous knot, every cell in my body crackling with anticipation. Why doesn't he call me? Or email me? Or text me? He said he would. Or better yet, knock down my door? Sweep me off my feet and carry me off to some deserted island where only the two of us exist. Far away from the fucking bitch.

I'm in love. Hopelessly, helplessly in love with Brandon Taylor. I think I've always loved him. From the first moment I set eyes on him. He's always been the master of my universe. But now, tonight in Cannes, he became the master of my soul. The part of me that's reserved for only sinners and lovers.

I am a new woman. I have sinned. And I have loved. With all my heart, all my body, and all my soul. Addicted to his dominant force, his dominant pleasure, I have broken a cardinal rule. Never sleep with your boss. Even worse, I've fallen hard in love with him. Ceded all control over my emotions, trespassed all physical boundaries, and defied my moral integrity out of lust and greed. Completely submitted to him with not a soupçon of regret. "It's complicated" is the understatement of the century. I want him so badly there's a knife in my chest.

Another hour passes. Still no word. My jet-lagged eyelids are as heavy as lead. The only thing that's keeping me awake is the ache between my legs. That persistent throbbing that won't go away. I'm losing hope, getting more anxious with each labored breath. Maybe he's gone back to stunning "It Girl" Katrina and is fucking *her* brains out right now. I shudder at the thought. Maybe I was a fly by night fling. Just his little fuck toy. Maybe all that stuff he told me about her was pure bullshit and all those lines he used on me were just lies. Pure acting. That explains why he never mentioned breaking up with her before this trip. My heart clenches at the possibility of deceit and even harder at the uncertainty of our future. He didn't after all say he loved me. So, he has feelings toward me. What does that mean? Maybe there's no difference between saying bring me my Starbucks and bring me to orgasm. Am I just a convenient doormat he can get off on?

With a sickening, sinking feeling, I finally doze off. A ping of my phone awakens me. I snap open my eyes and bolt upright. I glimpse the time—4:45 a.m.—and then go straight to my emails. My pulse sounds in my ears and my chest tightens against my breastbone. It's from Brandon! And marked *URGENT* in the subject line. My heart beats so hard, I can barely breathe. With a trembling finger, I open it.

> *I have no choice but to terminate your employment contract effective immediately. I expect you to honor your non-disclosure agreement and share nothing you know about my personal life with anyone, especially the media. If you fail to do so, I will be forced to take legal actions that will result in costly litigation.*
>
> *Please remove all your personal belongings from my premises as quickly as possible. Good luck with your future endeavors.*
>
> *—Brandon Taylor*

The words collide in my head like bumper cars, my emotions coming at me from every direction. So out of control, I hyperventilate. It takes all I have not to faint or vomit. I feel like someone's taken an ax to my heart and hacked it. Oh the pain! The guilt! I did it to myself.

I fell for him! No, I fell for his fucking act! The bastard! I hate him! But I hate one person more. No, not Katrina. Myself. Self-loathing mixes with self-pity. I allowed him to make me his fuck toy. I submitted. How naïve and gullible could I be? All along, there was never anyone except Katrina. Devastation devours me in a single gulp. I hit delete. Finally, another, more powerful emotion sets in. Sorrow. The tears finally fall. My greatest love has become my greatest loss.

Five numbing minutes later, my bag is packed. That's because I'm taking virtually nothing with me. All the stunning outfits, including the lingerie and accessories Brandon bought me, are staying behind. Maybe some hotel housekeeper will find them and enjoy them. Play dress-up in them and have her own Prince Charming fantasy that I hope will come true.

Battling my tears, I arrange for a flight home. The ticket is ridiculously expensive, but I don't care. I put it on my credit card. It's departing at eight a.m.

My hotel phone rings, and the voice of the concierge lets me know my driver is here. Do I need help with my bags? I tell her no and that I'll be down in a few minutes. My mind and heart distraught, I decide to write Brandon a note. It's more for me than for him. I need closure and some semblance of dignity. Sitting down at the desk, I take a sheet of the hotel's signature écru stationary and put a pen to it. Tears blur my vision.

> *Brandon~*
>
> *This is goodbye. Thank you for giving me the opportunity to work with you. The guesthouse will be cleared out by the time you get back to LA. You can be sure I will honor our non-disclosure agreement and treasure our time spent together.*
>
> *I will always remember you. You're unforgettable.*
>
> *~Zoey* ♥

By the time I add the heart, a regrettable after-thought, sobs are wracking my body. With quivering hands, I fold the letter and slip it into an envelope before my tears blotch it up. I cannot bear to write the words again.

With my roller bag in one hand and the letter in the other, I stagger out of my hotel room. At this wee hour in the morning, the elevator comes quickly and descends without stops to the lobby. While last night it was bustling, the lobby at this hour is all but deserted. Wheeling my bag, I trudge to the front desk. The lovely lady who checked us in is still there. This must be the end of her long shift. She's as cheerful as ever.

"Ah, bonjour, Mademoiselle Hart. Can I help you?"

"I'm checking out."

"Oh? Was everything okay?"

"Y-yes." I stammer, thinking of something that will explain my puffy, bloodshot eyes. It comes to me quickly. "I have a sudden emergency at home."

"I am so sorry to hear that. Would you like me to call a taxi to take you to *zee* airport?"

"Thank you, but I've arranged everything through the concierge."

A smile of approval curls on her face as I set my letter to Brandon on the counter. "Would you be kind enough to get this to Monsieur Taylor?"

"*Bien sur.* I'll have someone leave it under his door."

"Thank you very much."

With relentless, pulsing pain, I head to the hotel entrance.

Au revoir, Cannes.

Au revoir, Brandon.

Au revoir, forever.

FADE TO BLACK
END OF BOOK 2

UNFORGETTABLE 3
THE CONCLUSION IS AVAILABLE NOW!

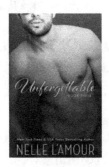

Brandon: I fucked up big time. She never wants to see me again. I may have a cock that belongs in a museum, but I'm the biggest dick in the world. My psycho fiancée, Katrina Moore, has got me by the balls. In just a few weeks, we're getting married live on TV. With my career on the line, I have no choice. I'm facing the most difficult decision I'll ever have to make. I'm damned if I do; damned if I don't.

Zoey: How could he do that to me? He used and abused me, made me his doormat. All the things he said and did to me were just an act. Stupid me for falling in love with him. He stole my heart, my body, and my soul. But there's one thing he's not going to take away from me—my dignity. There's a reason I don't own a TV. I can't bear to watch him say his forever vows to the woman he chose over me. Oh, Brandon Taylor... my dreammaker, heartbreaker. You'll always be unforgettable.

Hold on to your seats for the steamy, action-packed conclusion to Nelle L'Amour's bestselling new series. Be prepared to laugh, cry, and swoon!

THAT MAN
INTERNATIONAL BESTSELLING SERIES
WITH OVER 1000 5-STAR REVIEWS!

After you read *UNFORGETTABLE 3*, you may want to find out what really happened between scorchin' hot Blake Burns and crazy Katrina. My highly rated *THAT MAN* series is available FREE to Kindle Unlimited subscribers for the first time ever! Be prepared to laugh, cry, and swoon!

Note from Nelle

Dearest Lovely Readers~

I have been totally blown away by all your love and support. Your heartfelt reviews, emails, and Facebook messages have brought me laughs, tears, and big smiles. I have loved reading every word.

If you loved reading *UNFORGETTABLE 2*, I hope you will consider posting a review. The length doesn't matter. Even a short review means so much to me and can be so helpful to other readers. The links are as follows:

Amazon US: http://goo.gl/R4YyJu
Amazon UK: http://goo.gl/Pv1f74
Amazon CA: http://goo.gl/YaSmYy
Amazon AU: http://goo.gl/qWGSpU
Goodreads: https://goo.gl/1yG57G

I hope you'll equally enjoy *UNFORGETTABLE 3*, the steamy and suspenseful conclusion. Expect lots of twists and turns!!! And be prepared to laugh, cry, and swoon!

I hope you'll also check out my other books if you haven't yet read them and share your *UNFORGETTABLE* reading experience with your friends and reading groups. Please be sure to sign up for my mailing list and follow me on Amazon to be the first to know about my new releases, sales, and giveaways.

Newsletter:

http://eepurl.com/N3AXb

Amazon Author Page:

amazon.com/Nelle-LAmour/e/B00ATHR0LQ

Thank you again for all your love and support. It means the world to me!

MWAH!~Nelle ♥

Acknowledgments

I'm going to keep this short as there's a list that can fill a book at the end of *UNFORGETTABLE 3*.

A big shout out to the following:

- My amazing beta readers: Gemma Cocker, Kellie Fox, Kashunnah Fly, Kim Pinard-Newsome, Jennifer Martinez, Shannon Meadows Hayward, Adriane Leigh, Jenn Moshe, Sheena Reid, Karen Silverstein, Jeanette Sinfield, Mary Jo Toth, and Joanna Warren
- My personal assistant, Gloria Herrera
- My formatter, Paul Salvette/BB eBooks
- My cover artist, Arijana Karcic/ Cover It Designs!
- My proofreader, Mary Jo Toth
- My Release Blitz hosts, Kylie McDermott and Caroline Richard/ Give Me Books Promotions
- My family

Love you all. Couldn't do it without you!

MWAH! ♥

About the Author

Nelle L'Amour is a *NEW YORK TIMES* and *USA TODAY* bestselling author who lives in Los Angeles with her Prince Charming-ish husband, twin teenage princesses, and a bevy of royal pain-in-the-butt pets. A former executive in the entertainment and toy industries with a prestigious Humanitus Award to her credit, she gave up playing with Barbies a long time ago but still enjoys playing with toys with her husband. While she writes in her PJs, she loves to get dressed up and pretend she's Hollywood royalty. She writes juicy stories with characters that will make you both laugh and cry and stay in your heart forever.

Nelle loves to hear from her readers. Connect to her via:

Email:
nellelamour@gmail.com

Twitter:
www.twitter.com/nellelamour

Newsletter:
http://eepurl.com/N3AXb

Facebook:
www.facebook.com/NelleLamourAuthor

Amazon:
amazon.com/Nelle-LAmour/e/B00ATHR0LQ

Website (coming soon):
www.nellelamour.com

Books by Nelle L'Amour

Unforgettable

Unforgettable Book 1
Unforgettable Book 2
Unforgettable Book 3

Seduced by the Park Avenue Billionaire

Strangers on a Train
Derailed
Final Destination
Seduced by the Billionaire Boxed Set

An Erotic Love Story

Undying Love

Gloria

Gloria's Secret
Gloria's Revenge
Gloria's Forever
Gloria's Secret: The Trilogy

THAT MAN Series

THAT MAN 1
THAT MAN 2
THAT MAN 3
THAT MAN 4
THAT MAN 5

Writing under E.L. Sarnoff

Dewitched: The Untold Story of the Evil Queen
Unhitched: The Untold Story of the Evil Queen

CPSIA information can be obtained
at www.ICGtesting.com
Printed in the USA
LVHW021507280920
667305LV00002B/316